BLUE MOON

BLUE MOON

DAMIR KARAKAŠ

Translated from the Croatian by
ELLEN ELIAS-BURSAĆ

SELKIES HOUSE
LIMITED

INVERNESS

Originally published in Croatia as *Blue Moon* by Sandorf in 2014
First published in the UK in 2025

by

Selkies House Limited
registered at:
Elm House, Cradlehall Business Park, Inverness, IV2 5GH

www.selkieshouse.com

9 8 7 6 5 4 3 2 1

A CIP catalogue record for this book is available from
the British Library

ISBN: 9781917254267
ISBN E-book: 9781917254274
ISBN Audiobook: 9781917254281

This book was published with the financial support of the Ministry of Culture
and Media of the Republic of Croatia.

This book has been selected to receive financial assistance from English PEN's PEN
Translates programme, supported by Arts Council England. English PEN exists to
promote literature and our understanding of it, to uphold writers' freedoms around
the world, to campaign against the persecution and imprisonment of writers for
stating their views, and to promote the friendly co-operation of writers and the free
exchange of ideas. www.englishpen.org

Typeset in Adobe Caslon Pro by Carol Wombly @ Adobe Fonts.
Printed and bound in Great Britain by TJ Books,
Padstow, PL28 8RW.

PART ONE

PART ONE

A person I know, a rockabilly fan like myself, learned of his mother's death while he was at a salon, halfway through a haircut. I heard that my granddad had died while I was combing my hair.

I had just shampooed and was primping a new pompadour in front of the mirror when the phone rang and wouldn't stop. My father was on the line—he was calling from the post office and told me about Granddad.

I asked, "When's the burial?"

He said, "Come tomorrow and lend a hand."

Then he said, "And don't you dare come looking like you know what."

I called Eli to tell her about Granddad, that the next day I'd be going to the village where I'm from; she'd gone to stay with her mother the day before and she'd be there over the weekend. Back I went to the bathroom. I stood in front of the mirror for a while and thought some about Granddad, I looked at myself, or at the pompadour, in fact, which could be said to be in full bloom.

While I was studying, or to be perfectly honest, while I was not studying, the first thing I'd do at the dorm when I got up around noon, was to stand in front of the mirror, dip my hands in water, primp my pompadour.

Then I'd dress, pull on my leather jacket, work on the pompadour some more, and off I'd go into town. Straight by tram to the dormitories along the Sava River. At the stop by the dorms there was a mirror, a tall one, a little tilted. It suited me perfectly.

There I'd stand. When a tram pulled into the stop, I'd pretend to be walking toward it, but in fact it was the mirror I was walking toward. After the tram pulled away, I'd go back, and then do the same thing again when the next tram pulled in, like a film rewound a hundred times, and what a joy each and every time; when I walked toward the mirror it looked as if I were springing out of some other, far more appealing and engaging life.

I took Eli's compact and standing in front of the bathroom mirror, I checked the pompadour on the right, on the left, from behind, on all sides; it was dynamite, especially in profile. Lately, this was by far one of my finest; I had the biggest pompadour, hands down, in town, everybody envied it. For that I could mainly thank my hair—lush, black— I was always particularly proud of my hair.

Even when I was a kid, women from my village used to approach my mother to comment on my hair, their voices dripping with envy, "It isn't fair—a boy with a head of hair like that."

I squeezed out a little more gel, rubbed my palms together, slicked the sides down, and then a little more hair spray, shut my eyes, sprayed; a little more spray, and cemented it all gloriously into place.

Later I went to bed—one small pillow under the head, two larger pillows firmly planted, one on each side. I wedged my head with care between them, the huge ducktail, a gift from God, proudly jutting skyward.

Donning my Hein Gericke leather jacket, which I'd toiled for months to earn on construction gigs I got through the student job office, I laced my leopard-print creepers, tied a red bandanna around my neck, cinched the belt on my pants with the brass buckle, the one with the crisscrossed pistols, and smoothed my sideburns, their sharp points reaching almost to my lips.

I inserted my earphones, switched on the big, pale blue Walkman from East Germany I'd picked up one Sunday at the Hrelić flea market, and blasted away with "Stray Cat Strut."

Checking the pompadour one last time, I strode at a deliberate pace toward the tram stop—then the wind, one of my worst enemies, began to harsh my mellow. It wasn't gusting too hard, but when I reached the corner of a large building, my usual tactic was to stop, and then step with caution out into the open space, slowing the transition so the wind wouldn't muss my pompadour. This was one more tried-and-true methods, like the trick with the three pillows, for keeping a pompadour looking sharp.

I hopped onto the bus; people looked at me sideways, I don't care. It used to bug me but over the years I developed thicker skin and even started enjoying the way people on trams looked at me, laughed, pointed as if I were some sort of rare creature recently escaped from the zoo—there was a tinge of masochism to it all.

In the village where I'm from, people would just stare at me, amazed, but then, little by little they got used to it, they'd tease and sometimes they'd yell out to me from the local bar, threatening to rough me up, "so I wouldn't disgrace the village." Some of them, especially cousins, fled in panic, fearing I'd lost my mind.

There were drunks along the road who didn't even notice me. Punks they noticed, but rockabilly fans, never. They probably thought I was a mirage or something.

I am sitting on the back seat and stretching my long legs out in front of me. In the cloudy glass I keep an eye on the contours of the pompadour, the city I'm leaving behind, the morning lights.

I think about Granddad and his death. Lately he would often say, "When I can't live any more, I'll hang myself." As if preparing us.

The one surprising thing was that he didn't. He shot

himself with his M-48. He sat on a chair, leaned the rifle barrel to his chest, and pulled the trigger with his big toe.

When my father called to tell me about Granddad, he said, "This is the only smart thing he's done in his whole life." Then with fury in his voice he added, "His bloodstains are all over the house."

This immediately reminded me of the times when, as a kid, I'd be in bed, down with a bad case of the flu. Mama would tie cold beet slices to the hot soles of my feet to bring the fever down as fast as possible, so I could do something around the house with Father because he had no patience for the flu. Each time he walked through the yard he'd stick his head into the doorway and give an angry shout, "Whoever's not up to living, just go ahead and die, why don't you."

I started crying; I covered my face with my hand and cried silently—stripes of tears.

My granddad and Father were always wrangling over something. For a time they sparred because Father was the first in the village to get a squat toilet and dug the septic tank next to the house.

The toilet was in the outside hallway we called the "gank," and before the squat toilet we'd had a wooden latrine which was, in fact, just a heart-shaped hole cut in a board, and the shit would fall down through the heart hole and pile up right behind the house; and sometimes the mound of shit was so big, beneath the heart, that the tip of it almost brushed your ass.

It was worst during summer when the whole house stank from the latrine, and while you were mid shit, clouds of flies greedily swarmed your ass.

The house also smelled of dung, because the cattle were housed in the area right beneath us; there were only floorboards covered in linoleum between; but dung didn't have the same odor.

So, after the squat toilet was put in, Granddad decided to go shit in the stable in protest. The other big fight broke out over buying a television—one of the first in the village.

It seemed like Granddad was looking for more and more reasons to fight. He was out to spite Father who was behaving as if he were the one in charge, and didn't include him, Granddad, in his plans.

As to television, without a doubt Granddad most hated soccer; he insisted it was all a fake, that the players were rubber figurines running on electric power.

He loathed the advertisements. If a thing is worth anything, why advertise it? he said.

When I first showed up in the village with my pompadour, he found it quite unremarkable. A hairdo is a hairdo, he said, uninterested.

This further reinforced our alliance against Father, which was mostly Granddad grumbling about him, and me giving the occasional nod.

Granddad was a small man, bowlegged, always with his hands clasped behind his back. If someone's cow strayed onto our grass, he'd grab his axe, run after the careless young cowhand, hurl the axe at him; he was precise enough that he'd miss the kid by a meter or two. He loved flinging that axe.

Once, he threw the axe after his favorite cow when it strayed onto someone else's field. As she fled the blade sliced into the tendon of her rear leg; she toppled over on it and rolled, poor thing, like a big fleshy barrel, and this meant we'd have to butcher her. He sat down beside her in shock and sobbed long and hard, no tears, his whole body shaking.

Sometimes he would tell me about his own father; how they hadn't loved him because he thrashed them for no reason; one day his father pretended to be dead just to see if anyone in the house would weep to see him go. He faked hanging himself.

When the members of the household began to rejoice, he opened his eyes, climbed down from the noose and thrashed them all again.

I took off the earphones, left the bus, and set out on the winding road into the mountains. Along the way I ran into an old lady, all in black, with a basket perched on her head.

"Hello," I said.

She looked back at me and crossed herself three times.

After a while I stopped to catch my breath; apples were dropping from the trees, and as they fell onto a red-tiled roof they bounced off, rolled onto the paved yard, smashed apart and released a powerful scent. I bent over and stretched my hand through the iron railing, reached half an apple, bit into it, and walked on.

I listened to dogs barking back and forth to one another in the distance. Beyond the hill the first gables of the wooden houses began appearing; my village was beyond the next two hills.

I arrived in the dark early evening; the clouds were black and low. They pressed down on my head.

I climbed the freshly scrubbed wooden stairs, entered slowly, and saw my father sitting pensively by Granddad's coffin, lit by a bare light bulb. The kitchen was the largest room in the house and this is where they'd laid out my dead grandfather.

When he saw me, he rose slowly to his feet and stared, wordless, at my hair. He looked me right in the eyes—he seemed ready to slaughter me with that look.

Lightning flashed outside, then again, and the light bulb faltered for a few moments, flickered, went out.

Father made a move in the dark, pulled a flashlight out of the cupboard, lit me, then my hair. As if he still couldn't believe his eyes, he shuddered, shook his head, returned to the cupboard, and pulled out the kerosene lamp, lit the wick, cranked it up; the room swayed in the light.

I looked inside the open coffin; Granddad was covered from head to toe with a white homespun sheet; under the sheet his hands were crossed over his chest as if he were holding them over the hole left by the bullet.

I drew the sheet back from his waxy face for a moment. Under his moustache I noticed a smile, slight, barely there, just the corners of his mouth. I moved closer. He looked as if he'd died happy; he was probably sick of life. Maybe that's why he shot himself—he wasn't sick, as far as I knew, he tended the cattle in the forest above the house, every day, twice a day, in the morning and the afternoon.

He liked tending the cattle, he'd lie under a bush, cross his arms under his head, and with a piece of straw in his mouth he'd say, "As long as I don't have to be looking at that imbecile in the house."

I examined his moustache once more and then covered him. Because of the whiskers, he and Stalin always reminded me of walruses. Though he had nothing in common with Stalin, nor did he sport his whiskers to honour Stalin. This was his moustache, plain and simple. And besides, he hated the Russians. This was probably because one of his brothers was killed in the Ustasha units that fought at Stalingrad.

Granddad had been an Ustasha, too; they were all Ustashas in the village, except one who suddenly opted to go off into the forest to join the Partisans; this was such a disgrace that the man's father hanged himself that same day in his hayloft. Granddad claimed he never killed anybody during the war; I believed him. But one of his brothers, the youngest, killed everybody he could get his hands on: men, women, old people, children.

He especially hated Roma. He would mount them, horse-like, grab them by the hair, kick them in the sides as if spurring them to a gallop up a hill; when he'd ridden them to a bottomless pit, he pushed them in.

"You take after my youngest brother," said Granddad once, looking thoughtfully at my hair. "When I look at you it's as if I'm seeing him standing there. Your hair is just like that mane of his."

"But, Granddad," I said stopping in my game, "he murdered people."

Granddad winced, then gazed off somewhere into the distance.

"Not his fault," he muttered. "Satan was to blame."

Not long after this, I took the compact from Mama's handbag and went into Granddad's room. The door was unlocked; sometimes he locked it. He did not trust banks, so he preferred keeping his pension money locked in the drawer of his nightstand. I took the mirror over to Granddad's bed. Above it there was an enlarged, wood-framed photograph of five men, from the waist up: Granddad and his four brothers. All of them wore suits and ties, and they were lined up, almost crammed together, so Granddad—the first in the row—was the only one who could be seen with both shoulders.

My gaze came to rest on the last one in the row, barely more than a boy; Granddad's youngest brother.

I stared into the small mirror and then at the photograph, the pale face framed by lush, black hair. Then back at the compact; a ripple of fear shot up my legs.

Granddad's youngest brother and I were as like as two peas in a pod.

*

I rested my hand on the edge of Granddad's coffin. Father came over, brushed my hand off, looked up and glared again at the hair.

"What did I tell you over the phone?" he wanted to know.

"Where is Mama?" I said, evading an answer.

Father said, "Didn't I tell you not to come to the funeral looking like this?"

I looked over at Granddad, as if briefly seeking his support.

Father said, "Good-for-nothing, you failed at university, you've failed at life. Why not go ahead and kill yourself."

Again, I said nothing.

"Freak," he said. "People laugh at me over your hair. I can't go to the local bar because of your hair. I can't live because of your hair. And you have no respect for the dead, coming like this to the funeral."

"Granddad loved me," I snarled. "He hated you."

Father's eyes bulged sharply.

"And I hate you!" he shouted.

Then he punched me in the head.

The blow was unexpected, as if it had come from far, far away. I staggered back, then straightened up, looked at him in surprise.

He used to beat me often enough, he'd slap me with an open hand on the head, on the legs, flog me with a cane, with a belt, but never punched me with his fists. Maybe he figured he could have killed me with his fist when I was a kid. His fist would be raised above me, but he'd slap my head with his open hand. Anyone watching from the side when he was closing and opening his fist might have thought he was trying to impress very important thoughts deep into my mind.

He came a half-step closer and swung again. I ducked and his meaty fist swung through the air. He lunged forward, heavy—massive—as he was, and his hip jostled the coffin with Granddad inside and it wobbled a little, and he pressed me into the corner. He snatched me by the pompadour and a triumphant expression flashed across his features, as if he finally had me trapped.

"Eh, now you'll pay for everything!" he said and swung from above at my head. I ducked; he punched me anyway. Quickly my hands clenched into fists. Teeth. Eyes. When he swung again, I kicked him in the balls as hard as I could. He groaned, stepped back, his eyes bugged, and then, mustering my strength, so much so that the pompadour completely came undone, I punched him right between the eyes. Like a wind-up toy he swayed to the left, to the right, but stayed on his feet.

Father gawked at me, appalled, even more appalled than when he first set eyes on my pompadour. He clenched his teeth, and countless red veins branched on his neck, bulging to the point of bursting. He said, in a strangely soft voice,

"You degenerate, you raised a hand against your own father."

He went at it again, kicking and punching; we hit each other, grappled around the coffin, over the coffin, nearly tipping it over; we looked like drunken boxers.

Then he stopped and shouted, "Now you're done for, I'm going for the axe!"

I popped him once more right on the chin, then kicked him in the legs, he staggered and fell by the door; when he hit the floor, groping for a handhold, the house shook to its foundations. Outside the rain had just started. He lay there, bloodied, moaning loudly. I began kicking him with my left foot, my right foot, I stomped on him until he was flattened, and I was barely able to make myself stop.

Out into the rain I went, down the road, and began to cry uncontrollably. My hair hanging down, my arms hanging down, I strode along the road into town. Some kind of monster.

2

I was standing with Džimi by the bar at Podroom where the two of us always went on Saturdays for music. Some kids were performing at the club.

I nursed a beer and watched the girls, there were only three—ugly, only a mother could love them. Neither Džimi nor I had a girlfriend. I don't know whether he'd ever had a girlfriend. I also don't know where he got his nickname from. He probably gave it to himself, just like I did mine.

One Saturday I was on my way to Jabuka—a girl, a fan of punk rock, had invited me to the club for her birthday party—I stopped and through the darkness I could hear the music; I stood there and listened. Leaning against the nearest tree for a time, I closed my eyes and listened.

Down I went into the dive, which looked as if it had been excavated in the side of a hill by a giant mole, and I found myself surrounded by pompadours. A glittering disco ball spun below the low ceiling spilling light, and the pompadours looked like antennae directly connected to the very god of music; I watched the scene from a half-dark corner, listened to the music, and began to feel that after a thousand years I'd finally found my tribe.

Over time, I began going to Kulušić on Fridays for Blue Moon night, and then every Saturday it was Podroom. I began enjoying rockabilly music more and more; as if it wakened another me, someone from a past life. For this new life I had to come up with a moniker—I heard the jingle for Čarli dishwashing liquid and decided on Čarli.

I got to know Džimi right there at Podroom; he was standing like me, leaning on the tin bar, that's how we became close friends. He was a huge fan of Elvis. He never wore a leather jacket but one of those varsity baseball jackets and his pompadour was like early Elvis— combed, greased, and a lock of his hair often fell over his plump cheeks that looked as if he were holding two sizeable apples in his mouth. He once admitted he had been a punk rocker.

Then some guy told him that punk rockers can't be fat because the fatboy punker look is so wrong. Overnight he switched to rockabilly; now he says that without rockabilly music he can't imagine his life.

After the sweaty kids trotted out something of their own for their finale about a girl who's screwing her Doberman, and her boyfriend finds out and dumps her and she begs for forgiveness, DJ Zuluf played music, mostly local rockabilly bands: The Greaseballs, Torpedo...

After they parked their motorcycles with clangs and clatters, in came—the Vampires; there were a dozen of them and each had a good-looking girl with him, even gap-toothed Teks, a rockabilly fan who, as word had it, never wore underwear, but went commando.

As always, the Vampires took over their part of the floor, danced for a while, drank, and then left.

A fistfight broke out. Two of the rockabilly kids, Pinki 1 and Pinki 2, fought, kicked each other, and with their pompadours under the disco ball they looked like two roosters out to kill each other as quick as possible. Nobody was on security, so DJ Zuluf, once a junior Yugoslav boxing champ, stepped from the booth and shoved them out the door.

Later, a beautiful girl, about two meters tall, came in wearing leather pants; they called her Skyscraper. Two kids, psychobillies, came in, their heads shaved, only a lock of hair flopping over their foreheads. They were eating plums and spitting out the pits. DJ Zuluf noticed, kicked them both in the ass and chased them out.

At some point before morning, Džimi suggested we find some ćevaps. We slid and tumbled down the slippery green slope into town, each of us falling once. I landed easily on my hands, but when Džimi fell, with his hundred or so kilos I thought he'd never get up. He just groaned, pulled out the comb he'd inherited from his grandfather, fixed his hair and followed me; I was sure the ground would long show the dent from his body.

We walked into an all-night ćevap joint; a colorful crowd was there: punk rockers, metalheads, quasi-mafiosi, students—most of them wasted on drugs and alcohol—the boss rubbing his hands with glee.

I didn't like the ćevaps at this place because I'd heard that piles of dog hides had been found a few years before in the attic of a house on the outskirts of Zagreb, and that the owner had been mixing dog meat in with the meat for his ćevaps, but he managed to cover it up. I told Džimi about it not long before, but he wasn't worried; and besides, he was the only person in the world who actually drank a sandwich. When someone asked him what he was drinking, he'd often say: a sandwich.

We planted ourselves at the corner of the bar; Džimi ordered a big serving of ćevaps and a beer. For me—just a beer.

I held the sweating bottle and sipped at it, looking around the room; all the tables were taken.

"What did you like eating the most when you were little?" Džimi asked me with that growly voice of his.

"No clue," I said.

"Chicken wings for me!" he said, his mouth full.

Then he said, "The better to fly with."

I tried to imagine him flying, but all I could picture was a giant helium-filled balloon.

In the mirror, right next to my pompadour, I caught sight of a girl; she was sitting in a corner booth, working on a beer and staring out the window. She had red hair; if she'd lived in the Middle Ages she probably would have been burned at the stake for that hair. Several guys had crowded in around her, eating ćevaps, but they didn't seem to be with her.

I was looking at her in the mirror and snapped photographs of her with my eyes; then I shut my own eyes and for a while imagined myself sitting with the girl, like in a cowboy film, in a tin tub; she on one side, me on the other, our knees sticking up out of the water—mine pointy and hers rounded, the kind of knees women have who bear a lot of children.

When the guys got up and left, I picked up my beer and winked to Džimi. We went over to the table. Džimi sat across from her and I took the seat next to her. Other people came in, one of them perched on the edge next to me, pushing me a little closer to the red-headed woman. Local and foreign hits were playing on the scratchy-sounding radio with its antenna pulled out at an angle—just then it was the Beatles.

"So, may I ask you something?" I said softly in her ear.

She turned slowly, and drew back a little to see me better, because we were so close that our breaths met. Her face was pale, freckled, her eyes big and green.
"Who do you like more?" I asked. "The Beatles or the Stones?"

She gave me a look as if I didn't even exist, calmly took another sip of her beer, stood up, paid and left.

I just woke from a really bad dream; I am a bandit, actually the leader of a bad-ass gang, Billy the Kid is my friend, and Wyatt Earp is our sworn enemy.

I'm galloping on horseback with my gang, chasing golden-yellow stagecoaches all day long; I keep spurring on my horse. After a long chase over the prairie, we catch up and stop yet another of the coaches. The coachmen immediately throw down their Winchesters, they don't even use them, and better that they don't, they hold their hands high in the air, the travelers, terrified, clamber out, and line up one next to another, some clasp their hands behind their neck.

I take an empty Post Office sack and go slowly from one traveler to the next, I look them in the eye. Some throw in money—others, gold chains, rings—one sticks his fingers into his jaw in terror and drops his gold dentures into the sack.

In the end I reach a beautiful red-headed woman in a lady's hat and white gloves that reach all the way to her elbows—I look and cannot take my eyes off her. Then somewhere from the folds of her skirt she plucks a little gambler's pistol, a Derringer, and while I'm staring at her, petrified, unable to move, and, I should add, I am the fastest draw in the land, she calmly takes aim at my head. The bullet from the gun's barrel speeds toward me, it is getting bigger and bigger, it blocks my view. My head fractures from the bullet, a fracture that sucks me totally into hollow darkness.

When fucking, I liked fucking best from behind, then the missionary position but with my head up high so my pompadour was out of reach; when they were astride me, I held their hands or guarded my pompadour with my arms; with Eli, I fucked her in every position possible, no regrets about the pompadour. And besides, it's already three days old and I'll work a new one up tomorrow.

I went over to the window and had a look out. Two

cyclists were passing by, one heading straight for the other, each of them fatter than Džimi. The bicycles under them looked like kids' toys. They were cycling slowly along the concrete path, but when they came to the point where they had to veer to the side, they bumped slowly, barely touching. Their unbearably slow progress, the spinning of pedals, the moment they came into contact, all of it happened gently, silently, slowly, like a slow-motion film, but their fall was terrible; they fell at nearly the exact same time.

Eli woke up, rubbed her eyes and watched me looking out the window.

"Something out there interesting?" she asked me.

"Two cyclists collided."

After a while she said, "So any chance you know stuff about bicycles?"

"What needs doing?"

"I have a bike in the cellar from my grandmother, it needs fixing," she said. "And there's one from my grandfather for you."

I imagined myself on a bicycle, a rockabilly guy on a bike, and quickly said I don't like bicycles.

"But I'll fix up your grandmother's," I said.

I sat on the edge of the bed and moved aside a pile of letters on the table so I could set down my water glass; the letters were invitations for her grandmother to take part in contests for prizes even though she'd died several years before. I drank the water and then went to pour myself more.

When I came back, I stared again at her breasts; at her amazingly large nipples, pink, like wine-soaked corks.

"Eli," I said, "you have terrific nipples."

She smiled and said, "My mother has even bigger ones."

*

I took my Walkman from the pocket of my jacket, lay back down on the bed next to Eli, who was reading a book for one of her classes, put on the earphones. With my thumb I pressed the button, and the cassette began to turn. I listened, wiggled my toes, and when Crazy Cavan came and sang "Rockabilly Rules OK," I took one of the buds out of my ear and gently inserted it into Eli's. She listened patiently halfway through the thing, then with a barely discernable movement she removed the earpiece and smiled enigmatically.

I moved her earpiece over to my other ear, listened to the rest of the song, switched off the Walkman, set it down on the chair next to the bed, and in sweet languor pressed up close to Eli.

"I'd never have guessed that I'd fall in love with a rockabilly fan," she said.

"And why not?"

"Because they're rednecks." She marked the page with a pencil and tossed her book to the floor. Then she spryly vaulted over me and strode off to the kitchen for a drink of water.

"And rockabilly music is also so redneck."

"So, what, for you, isn't redneck?"

From the kitchen, she said, "Cohen."

I breathed deeply.

"Have you listened to him?"

"I have," I said. "He's even more boring than Bob Dylan."

She came back, vaulted herself back to the wall and pulled the sheet up over us.

"Listen to this sentence of Cohen's," she said. "Is there anything emptier than the drawer where you used to store your opium?"

We're quiet, we lie in each other's arms.

"Have you ever done drugs?" I ask her.

"Used to," she says.

"What?"

"Everything. You?" she asks.

"Nope!" I say.

"So, you're saying you never smoked weed?"

"I did that," I say. "But beer's better."

We fucked, and talked again about the night at the ćevap joint; or rather the daybreak when I first saw her red hair in the mirror.

Then the rainy Saturday when I ran into her again at Zrinjevac Park; she had a cold sore on her upper lip. I told her I'd never seen anyone whose herpes was so cute; she smiled and said the only reason she agreed for us to go for a drink was because she wanted to get out of the rain.

Then we talked a little about what we were studying; she said she had to finish her degree in English and Russian as soon as possible, she had only two more exams to go, and I said I had to finish my degree in agriculture as soon as possible, and I had only three exams to go. This was a lie.

I had two more years left to go, and in the time it had taken me to get this far I should have already earned my BA plus a master's. Besides (this I didn't tell her) I didn't even know if my student index—that served as both my university ID and my transcript—was even in workable shape, or whether I needed to go out and get a new one and make the rounds, entering into it all the signatures and grades from the professors whose courses I'd already taken and that had been listed in my old index. If I had to, this would be the end of me. The thing is that half a year before, my father came to Zagreb. The day before he arrived, he phoned the front desk of the dorm and they posted a message for me: "Your father arrives at noon." I thought I'd hide my index among my books. My excuse—I'd left it at the university administration where I was waiting for another crucial signature. But then I left it out, after all, on the desk, so he could see I had nothing to hide; Father was only semi-literate anyway. He wouldn't be able to make sense of all the stuff that was in my index; I couldn't keep up with half of it myself.

While I was waiting for him that day, I played some hoops not far from the dorm, on the basketball court by the high school on Križanićeva Street. Caught up in the passion of the game, I was maybe twenty minutes late for the meeting with my father.

When I hurried to my room, which was always unlocked, my father wasn't there, and on the desk was my index, stabbed straight through with a knife, the tip of which had even gone through the board of the desk.

It was a hunting knife with the scabbard in the shape of

an eagle. I had stolen it years before from a hunting supply store and kept it on one of the shelves for dishes; I was barely able to yank it out.

I don't know whether Father stabbed the knife into the index because he was capable, by some miracle, of decoding it, or because I wasn't there in my room at the time he'd set; but I was quite sure of one thing—he no longer trusted me or my studies.

If he ever had trusted me; he'd stopped sending money long before.

I was waiting for a tram on Republic Square and kept glancing up at the sky—the clouds were sodden, heavy, it looked as if even the strongest wind wouldn't be able to make them move.

But, better pelting rain than wind; I went over to the nearest bookstore, purchased a plastic bag—if it starts raining I can put it on my head, protect the pompadour.

I remembered I needed to buy a new can of hairspray and start counting my change; I kept the coins in one jacket pocket and the bills in the other.

The Borongaj-bound tram arrived, I got on, sat down, and continued counting my change and bills. I'd earned the money through the student job office; for two days I staggered around under sacks of flour, moving them from one truck to another with two students from Africa. Although several days had passed since then, every muscle still ached.

I stayed on the tram for five stops; at the sixth, inspectors—a woman and a man—got on. Luckily, right away, they ran into a guy who first pleaded with them that he had no money, no documents, then in a rage he stripped off his white wool sweater, pressed it into the confused inspector's hands, and said, "There, comrade, confiscate this."

The door swung open, I got off, and went on foot to Džimi's building, right next to the tram turnaround. I walked for two stops while glancing up at the sky, it was on the verge of rain.

I entered Džimi's building, got into one of the three elevators, and pressed the button for the eleventh floor.

I rang the doorbell, his mother, a large woman whose face was remarkably reminiscent of John Wayne's, opened. She worked as a typist at the Misdemeanours Court, and, as Džimi once told me proudly, twice she'd won the Yugoslav national championship in speed typing; I would never have guessed that this slow-moving woman, with her cigar-shaped fingers, was capable of such agility on a typewriter.

"Hello," I said. She nodded warmly and gestured with her head toward Džimi's room.

I went into the room, a tiny room done in colorful wallpaper. The bunk bed in the corner took up most of the space. As always, Džimi was sitting on the floor by his old turntable, listening to records.

I nodded in his direction and settled quietly in the other corner next to a large mirror that was pegged to the wall. For a while I listened to Elvis' voice, which Džimi was so immersed in that he didn't even say hello, showing me that I should feel at home in his room.

I sat there, listened to the music, then over my shoulder I eyed the mirror—nowhere did I look more atrocious than I did in that damned mirror at Džimi's. In fact, I was hardly visible at all. Džimi, in that mirror, looked thinner by half.

When the record finally stopped spinning, I pulled out 40 Deutschmarks in bills and handed them to him.

He said, stretching and yawning, "If you don't have it, no need to pay me back."

"I do," I said. "I'll return the other 40 next week."

Džimi works, he has a regular salary, so I sometimes borrow money from him. Though he earned good grades in school, he didn't feel like studying, so his father, one of the directors at the Končar factory, found him a job there— he worked on the assembly line, and his father hoped he'd change his mind and choose to study something.

Not long after this, Džimi's mother knocked, told me to come to the kitchen; I had been eagerly awaiting this moment.

I have an aunt in Zagreb, and a few times when I was ravenously hungry I went to see her, hoping she'd give me a decent meal. But every time when she asked if I was hungry, I'd say I wasn't—out of pride.

Džimi's mother never asked me anything, she just put food on the table and called me over.

All she'd say was, "Dig in."

I stood up, washed my hands, and went to the table.

Džimi's mother said, "Go ahead and eat, eat as much as

you like."

Džimi took a seat across from me and said, "The stew is delicious."

I ate slowly, holding back so I wouldn't slurp everything up in minutes.

"Mama," said Džimi.

"Yes, dear."

"Give me another plate."

"What for?"

"So I can eat."

"You just did," she said.

Then, while washing the dishes, she turned to me.

"Do you wake up at three in the morning and scrounge for food in the fridge?"

"No," I said, my mouth full.

"It's just because I'm starving," said Džimi.

"Control yourself a little," said his mother.

"Easy to say," said Džimi.

"It's not healthy," she said, probably for the nth time.

"It's not healthy to be starving either," he said.

A little irritated, he got up and fetched himself a plate, piling it to the rim with stew.

He licked his empty soup spoon and dug in.

His mother rinsed the soapsuds from a glass and shook her head in despair.

"Have some more," she said to me and glanced over at Džimi as if he were a lost cause.

"I can't, thank you, it was delicious."

She offered me her homemade elderberry juice; I downed

it quickly from a heavy glass.

Then she walked around the kitchen, cleared the table, pretended Džimi wasn't there; he had bent down almost to his plate, gobbling greedily; in the end he took a slice of bread and wiped the plate shiny clean with it.

Then as if we'd agreed, we stood up and for a few seconds I stared out the kitchen window.

I liked the view from the window of this apartment; I had never been in an apartment as high as the eleventh floor. Dinamo's stadium held my gaze.

Once when we were at Džimi's, we watched a match with the Yugoslav national team who were playing here at Maksimir. Whenever there was a goal, a howl of thrill rose from the throat of the stadium, yet on the televised version of the match the player had only just kicked the ball.

Džimi drank some water and back we went to his room. A little later his seven-year-old brother barged in, dressed as an American Indian; he was scrappy, as if no relation of Džimi's; in one hand he had a slice of bread spread with jam, in the other, a plastic pistol.

"Hands up," he declared and pointed his pistol at me, pulled the trigger and said, "Bang!"

I blew on my finger, made a gesture as if stowing my pistol in my holster, and said, "Once again I was faster on the draw."

"Well that's not fair," pouted the boy.

Džimi said, "As far as I know, American Indians don't carry pistols."

The kid fumed, "I do."

Then out he dashed.

I sat with Džimi, for a while we talked about girls and then a drizzle began outside. He told me about a girl who went to Kulušić on Fridays, but she didn't go on Saturdays to Podroom, and she had long blond hair and big tits.

"When the DJ plays 'Woolly Bully' she goes wild."
I told him I hadn't noticed her; he said he had to find out her name.

"Oh yes," he said. "And let me show you Eli's building."

He got up, called me to the window, raised the blinds and pointed across the train tracks at a neighborhood whose six-story buildings had corrugated metal facades. I got up, came to the window, and stared over his shoulder.

"The second building in the row; I don't know which floor she's on," he said. Then he briefly explained the history of Eli's neighborhood, which didn't interest me, but I let him talk. He said the buildings were built after the big Zagreb flood—he couldn't remember which year—so temporary accommodation was built to house the people and there it was still. He'd known Eli, that evening at the ćevap joint he even knew her name, but Eli, as she later told me, knew Džimi only by sight, from the stop they shared at the tram turnaround.

"We share the neighborhood, but the train tracks divide us so we were always at war with them," he said and told me about some unruly kids who lived near her who used to compete to see who could squeeze out the bigger hunk of shit.

"They slapped me around once for no reason," he said

and added, "she never hung out with those guys."

She always, he said, looked like she was in a world of her own.

"Now I'll tell you something about her even though maybe I shouldn't," he said.

"Tell me," I looked at him, curious.

"I wasn't going to tell you, but we're friends so I will. She dated this drug addict for a long time . . . Tall, good-looking. I think his parents moved to Germany to get him away from it all," he said. "Don't go telling her I told you."

"We're cool," I said.

Then, in silence, we each read comic books; Džimi liked Torpedo and I liked Corto; I leafed through the comic, but Corto began looking more and more like that druggie, Eli's ex, so I slowly closed it.

Džimi's father arrived soon after that. We heard him eating dinner in silence with Džimi's mother, how he plunked into his armchair, took out his newspaper, rustled with it, struck a match and lit a cigarette. I opened the door to say hi; he was sitting in the living room, next to a largish bust of Josip Broz Tito, the cigarette in his lips, reading the paper. He set the newspaper aside and asked Džimi's mother whether she'd given me something to eat.

"He ate," she said. "And he can have more if he likes."

"Thanks, I'm full."

When Džimi and I thought the rain had stopped, we decided to go out for a walk.

His father was watching television.

"How're your studies going?" he asked, switching channels

with his remote.

"Fine," I lied. "Nearly done."

"Any day now your friend is going to be an engineer, but as for you—no bees no honey, no school no money," he said to Džimi.

Džimi was leaning over, pulling on his boots, pretending not to hear, and he seemed to shrink at his father's look.

I said goodbye to Džimi's parents and thanked them for the meal. We took the elevator down, bought a couple of beers, stood by the damp bench in front of the toddler day nursery, and drank.

Between two sips Džimi decided to disclose yet another secret, asking me not to say a word about this to anybody. I was afraid that it might be more about Eli, but he said, "I'm buying a motorcycle."

"A motorcycle?"

"Yes, a bike," he said. "I've started saving."

The alarm clock woke me in my student room; exactly 4:30 a.m. I got up, dressed, primped my pompadour, buttoned my leather jacket up to my chin.

A student was studying in the bathroom. He was pacing from wall to wall, book in hand, his eyes shut, mumbling, and I felt a sharp stab of guilt.

I would so love it if I were able to study now, knuckle down and really pound the books, but studying would no longer be enough for me to catch up. Should I sign up for a brand-new course of study? Start from scratch? I was really beginning to wonder, what will become of me? Then I felt a welling of panic.

I took a tram to the Student Center. My goal was to get a good number for my place in line so next week I could sign up for a new job. When I got there at daybreak there were already some thirty people waiting; some of them were lying on the steps wrapped in blankets.

I stood in line, counted the people in front of me once more—thirty-four. Not bad, I felt sure a job would turn up for the next week. All I had to do was come every day and wait patiently. That was the biggest challenge. And every Friday I would have to register again.

For a while now I'd been hoping for a five- or six-day gig, but most of the jobs like that were given to people who knew someone. Here in the waiting room the jobs you usually got were for one or maybe two days. The female students mostly got cleaning jobs; the guys—loading and unloading.

Last week by some miracle I landed a job though my number had been #127; a guy came in, said he was unloading flour, it was Tuesday, some with higher numbers had decided to wait for a better opportunity at the end of the week, and there were no others around so I opted for that one.

At exactly 7 a.m. a bald man opened the door, let us in and began distributing numbers. I was given number thirty-nine—people must have elbowed their way in while I was dozing on my feet. I didn't complain.

I knew that Eli's mother was there in the apartment because as I approached the building, I saw her red Renault 4 with the dented front wing. She was standing by the window, holding a shopping bag, about to leave. I greeted her and kissed Eli loudly on the lips, as if defying her mother.

I didn't like her at all; maybe this started when she told Eli I had the look of damaged goods. Eli swears to me her mother was joking, but, though I tried to brush this off, whenever I saw a drinking glass, I'd imagine it cracked and that would remind me of those words of Eli's mother and again I'd smart with rage.

"How was it?" asked Eli.

"Where?"

"At the Student Center," she said.

"I got number thirty-nine."

"You'd be better off applying yourself to your studies," said her mother, a retired literature professor; Eli's late father was also a teacher. I hope Eli didn't tell her how hopeless my situation was with the way my studies were going.

When I admitted my lie to Eli after I told her I had only three exams left, she asked me in a calm voice never to lie to her again, and I asked her not to say a word about my standing at the university to anyone. She promised she wouldn't.

Eli asked, "Are you hungry?"

"No," I said, and waited for her mother to leave.

"Mama made some borscht."

"What's that?" I asked.

"A traditional Russian dish," said her mother, as if she

had asked me a question in school and then had given me the answer after marking me down with a failing grade.

"Let me have a taste," I said.

Eli got up, served some of the borscht in a plate, sliced some bread. I tried it, there were all kinds of things here, beets, meat; it suited me just fine, but I didn't want to show her.

I ate, feigning indifference. Her mother went on watching me out of the corner of her eye, though she pretended to be looking out the window; this rubbed me the wrong way. The way she looked at me was often distrustful, even when she had a kindly smile. Maybe the woman was right; even my mother has sometimes said, "I pity whoever hitches a ride with you in your cart."

I finished off all the food and took the dish to the sink. I went back to Eli, who was lying down with her leg bent, massaging her foot; her mother stood there for a while longer in silence, as if she wanted to say something, then finally she left. Luckily, she doesn't come by often.

"You don't tolerate my mother," said Eli, and stretched out her leg.

"I do," I said.

"Come on, get over that stupidness once and for all," she said. "Don't be a hick."

"Who cares about that," I said, taking care that my gaze didn't light on a glass anywhere.

Then the phone rang; Eli got up and brought the receiver to her ear.

"For you," said Eli.

"Who?" I got up.

"Your mother."

I'd given Mama Eli's number not long before and told her to call me there only in an emergency.

I grabbed the phone right away and asked; "What's up?"

I stretched the phone line as far as it would go and went to the farthest corner, and Mama told me what was up—they were going to have to dig up Granddad and bury him again.

According to her, their uncle from Australia hadn't been able to attend the burial (because he's an Ustasha) so he sent Father money for the funeral, and in return Father was supposed to send photographs of the burial to him in Australia. Father, she said, took his instant camera, which he'd bought years before, tried clicking it, but not a single picture popped out. Right there on the spot, she said, he smashed the camera, cursing the salesman and the photo shop.

Now Father wanted to re-do the burial and this time he hired a professional photographer from town.

Then in a weepy voice she said she knew we'd fought, but it would be a huge disgrace for the family if I missed Granddad's funeral twice.

Then, like always, she started in with the advice—I needed to think of the future, I should come decently dressed and have a normal haircut, and between the sentences she kept interjecting, "You're not a five-year-old kid anymore."

I held the phone to my ear and watched how, outside, a car was towing another car. And stopped listening to her.

*

Father showed up one day with a camera he'd bought in Rijeka. It was the black plastic instant kind, surprisingly light, and it popped out color photographs. He took one right away in the yard; a picture of the ox he had just led out of the barn, to see whether the camera was working properly.

Then he held the blank photograph which ceremoniously emerged from the apparatus. He heightened the ceremony with his self-satisfied expression and held the picture facing the sun until the blurry outlines of the animal first appeared on the paper, and after another ten seconds we had a color photograph of the ox staring, startled, into the lens.

After that Father put the camera up on the wardrobe in the bedroom as if it were some sort of totem; nobody was allowed to touch it. He'd just dust it carefully once a year, saying he was saving it for my wedding day; he only had a facial expression like that, brimming with focus and joy, when he ran a dust rag over his gun.

Around then our neighbor Marko bought a black-and-white television set, the first in the village, and every evening half the village would crowd out of curiosity into his house where, on a pine board attached to the wall, in the dark of the room, the television gleamed, casting shadows. Our neighbor Marko gave himself the right, as the set was his, to announce every few minutes, "Quiet now!" though we were already quiet. Again, he'd say, "Quiet, quiet." And we'd go on being quiet.

Mostly, when people finished their farming or other tasks,

in the evening they would flock, heeding an unwritten rule, to the "village cinema". The older ones sat on chairs, benches, the ottoman, and we children sat on the floor, while our neighbor Marko, with an expression on his face as if he were Nikola Tesla, would triumphantly press the "on" button, and, after a few seconds of waiting, across the screen would pour the magic image.

I loved movies; one day it occurred to me that I might try to make my own. When Father and the other members of the household weren't around, I climbed up on the chair, grabbed the camera, tucked it under my shirt and went out to a neighboring hilltop, my heart pounding against the camera. I stood atop the hill, looking down on the village, under the sun, beneath tall trees whose green peaks soared skyward.

I dropped my pants and underwear to my knees, sat in the grass and began jerking off with one hand, while snapping a picture of my crotch with my left.

Then, while still pulling the foreskin up over the tip, high above my head I held the photograph that had just emerged from the camera; I watched how the cock appeared from the ashy color. I felt as if everything that was momentarily happening was someone's higher will.

I kept jerking off the whole time, snapping pictures, then I set down the camera, arranged the pictures next to one another. On the last one, the ninth, which I timed to snap just as I was climaxing, the only thing you could see was a blurry splotch, like a snuffed-out sun.

I wiped the camera off on the grass, because I'd sprayed it with a lot of sperm, I had another close look at the nine photographs, then for a while I imagined them speeding up in sequence, one after another.

I piled them up, took them to the closest bush, scrabbled a hole in the ground with my fingers, laid the photographs in it and covered them well with dirt, grass, branches, so nobody could ever find them.

I wiped the camera off once more with grass, at home I wiped it with a damp cloth and, when nobody was looking, I put it back up on the wardrobe, checking several times, gauging whether it was sitting precisely to the millimeter on the spot where it had been.

3

I walked to the bus station, then set off from there for my home village. I was wearing a black leather coat that reached my heels. I'd combed my hair back with gel, smoothed my sideburns.

I put on dark glasses, eyed myself in a shop window; I looked like one of those terrorists from the 1970s—but I liked the look. A little later I sat on a tattered seat, they were all like that. There were another five people on the bus. I'd forgotten to bring my Walkman, so the bus driver tormented me with his music. The refrain of one song stuck in my mind, "I had a hundred women. Who knows how many there were."

I emerged from the belly of the bus, stepped into the empty center of the small town, and then the hour and a half on foot to our house. The day was long since dark.
I walked down the macadam road; when I entered the deep forest full of hooded trees, I made a lot of noise so I'd feel less frightened. From a distance I could hear the grumbling of dogs, and then the baying of a wolf, so I sped up. I walked at a rapid pace through the dark, down a road I'd walked along

countless times, and swung my arms to quicken the pace; as if I were seeking a path through the dark with my arms.

As I approached my village, the dogs started barking again, yanking on their chains; I entered the pitch darkness of our yard, and its density made the snarling of my dog, Medo, seem even louder. He didn't recognize me at first and there was something sad about that.

"Hey, Medo!" I called softly in the direction of his doghouse where he was leashed, and he stopped.

I groped for the edge of the house and climbed the stairs to the upper door; it was locked, but the key was in the lock. I turned the key twice, entered, and switched on the light.

On the upper floor I was alone, my parents were sleeping on the ground floor; I heard Father snoring. I imagined his M-48 next to him, the one Granddad killed himself with; at night he always kept it by the bed in case a bear, wolf, fox, or other animal strayed into the yard. A few years ago, a wolf took our dog from the tether. All that was left on the chain was a clump of bloody hairs.

I'd never had my own bedroom, so I chose a room that was free; as always, the little room with the military folding cot reminded me of my tiny student digs. I did not venture into the next room where Granddad and Granny had slept, where the photograph of Granddad's brothers hung. I was scared; he'd only just died.

I stood for a time and gazed out through the casement window into the dark; each time I inhaled I'd feel as if I had less air to breathe; this often happened when I came home. There were several old, abandoned houses in the village, and the silence was so great that I could hear how the sand was slowly dribbling from them, as if from an hourglass.

I stripped off my boots, pants, jacket, and crawled into bed under the army blanket; Unable to sleep, I listened to the occasional sighs of the cattle, so like human sighs. They reached me from the barn, no longer beneath us on the ground floor but some ten meters away, separated by the concrete farmyard—yet I could hear them.

Like a wet dog in warm hay, I curled up in my thoughts and fell asleep.

Soon I woke and couldn't fall back to sleep; I went on listening to the cattle in the barn, standing next to one other, occasionally locking horns.

In the morning, as always, I was jolted awake by a colorful barrage from Father; nobody had oaths more fanciful than his. "Fuckin' Jesus on a grain of wheat. Fuck your daily bread, slice by slice . . ."

He was of the opinion that if you don't curse God, you don't believe in him. And ever since he paved the farmyard in concrete, he had been cursing even more. When he took the cattle out each morning to graze, he didn't want them dropping dung on the short stretch from the barn over the paved yard to the forest path; but as if out of spite they planted a cow pat every single time just as they were ambling over the concrete.

I got up, collected my clothing that I'd strewn around the room, glanced out the window; Father was cursing and punching the cattle in a frenzy with his hand, his fist, kicking them to hurry them along. He circled them, trying to catch the steaming dung with his shovel. He was managing well, he'd probably become adept at it, but one wily cow was quicker. He angrily shooed the cattle to a nearby meadow and tethered each of them to a spike with a long chain, prepared in advance.

He came back and shot a glance at the little window of the room where I'd slept, and automatically I shrank back, as if he were shooting at me. Then he took his twig broom, cursed, and cleaned the paved farmyard.

When I came downstairs to the yard I encountered him, caught his vulpine profile out of the corner of my eye, but we walked by each other as if invisible.

I went into the kitchen and shook Mama by the hand; never had there been kissing, not between me and my mother, nor me and my father, nor between the two of them. I don't believe my father and mother had ever kissed each other on the lips; if they had, it's more than I can bear to picture it.

Mama had already set out a generous breakfast on the table: homemade sausages, eggs, bacon, prosciutto, home-baked bread—its shiny crust smeared with eggs, and in a big white pot there was freshly boiled milk.

Mama watched me while I ate, something I don't like, and she munched on the soft part of a piece of bread, while picking at the crust and tossing it to the cat. Luckily she didn't say a thing, gave no advice; but she was relieved to see I hadn't shown up with my pompadour.

All of a sudden, she kicked the cat in the gut; the cat flailed with its legs and fled in terror.

"Don't do that," I snapped.

"All they do is hump, yet there's mice everywhere," she answered, looking at the cat as it scampered off.

I ate and kept an eye on Father who was standing right by the window. With his hammer he was straightening old nails on the anvil, holding them between his lips while he worked. Then the neighbor, Mijo, stopped by and asked him, "So where's our engineer?"

He has been calling me that in front of my father ever since I started elementary school, buttering him up, because Father often lent him farming tools. Scowling, Father gestured toward me with his head, indicating that I was indoors, and went on pounding away with force at the rusty nail, probably imagining me on that anvil in its place.

Mijo had a family of eight, Josipa was the eldest and I knew her best of all his brood; several more villagers arrived shortly after this, and Marko, our neighbor, the one who got the first television, eyed me and said I looked taller to him than when he'd seen me last, six months before. A little later Slavo, a cousin, showed up. He had recently come back from serving in the Yugoslav People's Army. We hugged and he clapped me on the back, which made me draw in my shoulders.

"Now you look like a proper man, and not that haircut and the red bandana around your neck like you're still a pipsqueak, goddamn it, in the Pioneers," he said.

Finally, my father came inside. He explained, without looking at me, that the re-run of the burial would happen at two o'clock that afternoon.

*

I climbed up to the sooty attic and rummaged around in my cardboard boxes, finding some photographs. One was a class picture. All I needed was somewhere to lie down, so I positioned myself under a cracked roof tile that let clusters of golden rays shine through, and I studied the photograph. Images percolated.

When I was a kid, I preferred gazing at the class picture of 5A to this one of 5B, because Slobodanka was in 5A. Boba, we called her. My first love.

For a long time, I gazed at her eyes which flashed from the photograph as if they would burn right through the paper, her short dark hair combed to the side, her blue smock with the coat of arms of our school on it; we looked like little Chinese laborers.

Once, while I was head over heels in love with Boba, my parents had to take a cow to be serviced by a bull, and the owner of the bull lived near town. In these situations, when a cow is led a longer distance, two men take her, one in front with the halter, and the other behind, driving her with a switch.

Father and Granddad agreed (this may be the only time they'd ever agreed) that I would be the one to drive her with the switch, while Granddad would lead the way with the halter. I was horrified. I would be walking right through the center of town with the cow, and if Boba, who lived in town, were to see me driving the cow along the road, I'd die of shame. But Father and Granddad were implacable, the shape of their lips, tightly pressed, let me know they wouldn't be changing their minds.

When we set out, I pleaded the whole way with Granddad for us to take a detour around town via the fields, to avoid the town center, saying this was the shorter route, even though it was, in fact, farther. After my persistent pleas, he agreed, but once the bull had provided his service, Granddad decided, not to be dissuaded, that on the way back, before we turned onto the road heading off to our mountain village, we'd drive the cow along the main road. He had something he needed to ask the veterinarians.

Somewhere near school, right by Boba's building, I saw her. She was with her girlfriends playing dodgeball. My knees buckled, I tried to crouch behind the cow, I even thought of leaping onto the cow and swinging down behind her, the way Indians did in the movies.

But I was spotted. Her friends burst into giggles, pointing at Boba as if it were her fault that I was driving a cow through town. I looked at Boba, hoping for her support. But she looked as if I'd somehow betrayed her.

After the stop at the veterinarian's I cried the whole way home. When Granddad asked what was wrong, I lied and said my tooth was hurting.

Then I clutched the switch tighter and began really thrashing the cow, as if this was all her fault, until my granddad told me to take up the lead while he walked behind her.

I smile and study the photograph again after who knows how many times I've studied it. I'm sitting there in a blue smock, my gaze anxious; as if this gaze were photographed at the very moment, when I, while driving the cow, on the road, had caught sight of Boba and her friend.

I have a look at others in the photograph; in the back row, first from the left is Zdravko, my best friend at elementary school. When we went outside for recess, I'd drink a Coke and Zdravko would have a Pepsi; I much preferred Coke—it had a stronger taste and the shape of the bottles was more curvacious.

I decided to take home one of the bottles shaped like a female figurine and drink the Coke there, believing it would be an entirely different experience to drink the Coke in my village from drinking it in town. The next day I bought a Coke and though I was supposed to return the bottle to the shop after I'd drunk it out in front, I chose not to.

I left for home on foot with the bottle, not waiting for the school bus—I carried it in my hand like a relay baton or, better yet, an Olympic torch.

Somewhere halfway home I developed a fierce thirst and had a sip; after each sip my thirst only grew worse. I managed to hold off until I got home and put the Coke in the fridge. More than half of it was left and I planned to finish it off once my thirst became unbearable, to make the pleasure of drinking it all the greater.

I took my ball and began throwing it at a basket made from a stripped bicycle wheel, tied to a tree; I chased the ball under the improvised basket that was difficult to miss, and kept thinking about that bottle of Coca Cola, and the blessed moment when I'd finally drain it to the last drop, with the bubbles prickling my nose and eyes.

After I'd reached the point where I was so tired that I could barely stand, I abandoned the ball in a bush and headed, all sweaty, back into the house. COCA-COLA, COCA-COLA, COCA-COLA, my heart pounded from exhaustion, from the thirst and the thrill.

When I entered the kitchen, there was my grandfather standing by the fridge, like in some future Coca Cola ad, tipping the bottle back, draining it to the last drop.

Slavo was digging on one side, I on the other; the dirt piled up around our feet. Soon, almost simultaneously, our shovels hit the ready-made coffin, the hue of golden rust, narrowing at the feet. We pulled the coffin up out of the grave and sat down, sweaty and tired, next to it—an unpleasant stench was already wafting from within and a few minutes later it began reeking with more pungency.

Father came over (he probably assumed he'd still be able to take a picture of Granddad), and skillfully wielded the hammer claw to extract the nails and pry open the coffin. Granddad's corpse was seething with worms; I almost threw up, and after this scene which sickened us both, Slavo jerked his head away and went to the bushes to piss. Quickly Father closed the coffin lid and nailed it shut again, spitting next to it after every hammered nail. Then he pulled a rag from his pocket, thoroughly wiped the lid, then over it he threw a white, starched towel; he did all this with his face averted.

After ten minutes or so, a horseshoe-shaped cluster of people was standing around the grave and the coffin; they were conversing loudly and some of them were holding their noses. Father kept looking up, expecting the priest and the photographer, but the only person to arrive was my sister with her husband and young son in a sailor suit. My sister is older than me, she is married and lives in the nearby town.

I greeted them and patted my nephew on his hair.

Uncle Tome, who lived in Rijeka, drove up to the cemetery in his white Mercedes. The confirmed bachelor, as Father taunted him in front of Mama—over forty and still not married.

Father was growing edgy, pacing around the cemetery, cursing and kicking around at random, and finally the priest appeared. A few minutes later the photographer arrived so the burial could be performed.

In his hiking boots, the photographer buzzed around like an irksome fly and kept snapping pictures; the priest opened his book and read, slowly, as if listening to every word.

Before Slavo and I lowered the coffin back into the grave, the photographer jumped in and took a few quick photos from below. With a nimble hop he prompted Father to take a handful of dirt and throw it into the grave; they repeated this several times. Then Father gave Slavo the nod for us to lower the coffin and start shoveling the dirt because the stench had become nauseating. Two women were retching, and my little nephew threw up violently, so hacked with coughs that he bent over as if about to snap in two. We worked hastily, gagging on the acrid air, and finally used the shovels to smooth the mound. The photographer recorded the smoothing with professional finesse.

I set my shovel down and sat on the handle to catch my breath; my heart was pounding in my throat from the exertion. Slavo thrust his shovel into the dirt and leaned his full weight on it.

"Who'd have guessed that you're so skilled at digging," he said. "Yet you're the one who always has a book in his hands."

"I enjoy physical work."

"That's because you know you won't have to spend your whole life wielding a shovel," he said.

Slavo left, and a little dazed, I stared at the two crosses, Granddad's and Granny's, as if hers was tipping ever so slightly toward his, as if she were whispering something to him; then I went to join the others. I looked up at the gateway to the cemetery and, framed by the gate, I saw Slavo and Josipa who wore a black suit with a long black braid tossed over her shoulder. Though only sixteen, dressed as she was in black, she looked a lot older. I shook my muddy legs, walked over to them, said hi to Josipa, whom I remember as a reticent girl, and tossed the shovel over my shoulder. While the three of us walked toward the village and chatted, or rather Slavo talked, said he wanted to buy a new car but couldn't decide whether to go for a new or a used one, I stole glances at Josipa's generous hips when she turned for a moment and plucked a flower along the road to sniff it. Her perfect bottom, her breasts pulling taut the black cloth of her blouse, her big juicy lips—she'd matured into an incredible beauty. The kind of female beauty that is a little dizzying.

*

Slavo invited me over for a dinner of roast hare. He also invited Josipa; he was in love with her, but she was having none of it. Mama told me this the night before. Josipa showed up dressed in a dark-blue sweater that reached all the way to her knees.

A tin rooster spun on the roof; it looked as if it might speak at any moment with a human voice and reveal that, again, I had a hard-on for Josipa. Quickly I slipped my hand into my pocket and nudged my cock over so it would swell in a way that wouldn't be visible.

Slavo's father, my uncle, Krste, was already sozzled. He offered us home-brewed šljivovica. When we declined, Josipa asked for juice and I asked for water. With a chuckle he said, "Even in your shoe, water won't do."

He toddled over with a glass of water for me and served Josipa store-bought orange juice, diluted with water. He invited her to come with him into the new part of the house with its plaster walls—as yet unwhitewashed—so he could show her, as he said, the new tongue-and-groove wainscotting Slavo had installed himself and painted.

Not long after, a light-blue van pulled up by the hedge and out of it stepped Miško the Roma and his two young sons—curly-haired, wheat-yellow, sweet puppies.

Wearing a rumpled black blazer with padded shoulders, Miško shook hands with me to convey his condolences, and prodded the two boys to shake my hand, which they did, then he added, beaming with pride, that he had been there at both of Granddad's burials and that our village would never have a finer man than Granddad. Miško adored my grandfather, because Granddad had saved his father's life during the Second World War.

Just before the end of the war, Granddad returned for a few days from the area around Sarajevo where his unit had been stationed, and the Ustashas had taken Miško's father prisoner and brought him to the village. Granddad's youngest brother had already climbed onto Miško's father's back and was about to throw him into the bottomless pit when Granddad intervened.

Miško knew every detail of this story and he often told it—how my grandfather slapped his youngest brother in the face in front of everybody, then his brother drew his pistol and threatened Granddad, so Granddad slapped him again, hard, and after that they never spoke to each other.

Miško gestured for me to go with him behind the van where nobody could hear us, and he shooed away his sons.

"I wanted to tell you, I sold my horses and bought this little van," he said. "Now I'm getting ready to have my own company, I'll collect scrap metal, to begin with I'll have one worker, and later we'll see, so I chose a cousin, a strong boy, I'll pay him a hundred Deutschmarks a month, and if he's good, I'll give him a 10 percent cut, so now you tell me, you've got the book-learning, how much will the 10 percent come to?" he said, fiddling with his greasy hat.

Though I am no wizard at math, or figures, I did whasssst I could to explain to him that first he had to know how much he'd be earning, because only then could he calculate how much 10 percent would come to, but he wasn't listening. Instead he was cursing his young sons.

And besides, he was drunk. When he's drunk, my mother said, sometimes he beats his wife and shouts at the top of his lungs that his sons aren't his, because they're blond and he's dark-haired, and when he's sober, he is forever hugging and kissing them.

Last time I saw him he told me he loved them so much that he was always pretending to read the newspaper when he was in town, though he was illiterate, just so nobody would think that their father didn't know how to read. He gave me a farewell clap on the shoulder, herded his boys into the van, started it up and, steering with one hand, drove off in a cloud of exhaust fumes.

Not long after that Slavo showed up from somewhere, freshly shaven, wearing blue worker's overalls, a yellow folding ruler protruding from his side pocket. He perched with us on the edge of the well and started talking, as if reading from an invisible pad. First, he spoke in a pompous tone about his experiences in the Yugoslav People's Army, then he turned in particular to me, who would have to go, like he said, once I'd graduated.

Slavo was a year older than me. He loved to give speeches though he had only barely completed his locksmith training;

he often remarked that Tito had also trained as a locksmith and then went on to become president. At the mention of Tito my grandfather would scowl and look away.

Then Slavo began talking like a political commissar—about the precarious Yugoslav political situation, how everybody was choosing sides, the Albanians on one, the Serbs on another, the Croats on a third, the Muslims on a fourth. One of his eyes was trained on Josipa, the other on all the rest of us. When speaking about the political situation, the Croats and Serbs, he mentioned the neighboring Serbian Orthodox village, Crni Lug, where Boba's father was from. Her father was in charge of the police station in the town.

"Do you know that fellow, Đoko, who went through school with me in my class?" he said.

"The one you said had a Serbian flag stowed away in a cupboard?"

"That's him," he said. "I have heard that he recently attended a Red Star–Partizan match in Belgrade and brought back a big sack of dirt from Serbia. He poured it out all around his house and then declared that his home is on Serbian soil."

"Do you think that's true?" I said.

"One hundred percent," he said, with his eye still on Josipa.

"Then report him to the police," I said.

"Which police when they all come from his village?" he said. "I'd end up being the one arrested."

After this Slavo went down to the cellar and brought up a nice white hare, carrying it by the ears. With the hare in hand he looked like a magician about to perform a sensational trick out in his yard.

He held the hare by the ears and yanked on it hard, as if gauging its weight; a squeaky sound came out from between the hare's ears, like the long whistle of a locomotive.

Uncle Krste piled more wood into the blazing outdoor stove. Slavo went on holding the hare by the ears, then, looking away, he whacked it on the back of the head with a karate chop—the hare arched back, squealed, struggled to pull free. Slavo looked at it in amazement, shocked that it was still alive.

Then he looked over at Josipa, bewildered, as if apologizing, and then angrily at the hare which hadn't died from the first blow.

Again, he whacked it with all his might with another karate chop in the same place, and again, the hare survived; it squealed and wriggled. Bloody ooze pulsed from its snout, and Josipa turned her head away and covered her ears.

Infuriated, Slavo went on whacking the hare with a barrage of karate chops to the back of its head, keeping an eye on the tracks of his blows, and after each new blow the hare grew even livelier; its eyes swelled up so much that they looked like amber plums, if there even is such a thing.

"For God's sake, cut its throat," said Uncle Krste, losing his patience.

"When I decide something, then that's how it will be," said Slavo bitterly and looked again over at Josipa, who by now had dropped her hands but was still staring sadly off at the clouds.

He went on whacking the hare with karate chops to the neck, below the neck, the head, the belly, until finally the hare went still. Then Uncle gave him a sharp knife to skin it; but as soon as the tip of the knife pierced the hare's fur, it came alive again, and Slavo, clutching at its hind legs, was barely able to keep it from getting away; this time the hare wriggled so hard that it seemed as if it wished it could escape its own body. Then Slavo grabbed it firmly by its hind legs and slammed it against the wall; the blow popped one of the hare's eyes right out.

He sliced through the fur, skinned it, and when he had finally pulled the fur up over the head and then placed the blue-red skinned hare on a tray and into the oven, the hare's hind legs were still twitching.

"Well, goddamn this fucking hare!" said Slavo straightened up, exhausted, and wiped his bloody knife blade with a rag. "When I was in the army, I killed one with a single blow."

After I'd spent the whole morning carrying bags of cement on my back, at around 2 p.m. I was standing, bent, at the tram stop.

I went over to a nearby decorated shop window to have a look at myself, but the sun was beating down so hard that it looked as if I'd burn up in the reflection; my hair was filthy, full of dust, I could hardly wait to work up a new pompadour.

When I arrived at Eli's apartment, I fell asleep before I even sat properly in the armchair. Eli pulled off my boots and covered me with a blanket.

I slept, woke up with both hands tucked under my head. My stiff armpit hairs poked out and smelled rank. I got up; Eli was watching television; her red hair was piled under her head like a pillow; I kissed her and went to the bathroom, showered, dried my hair.

I came back to Eli, gave her a hug.

"How was work?" she asked.

"Backbreaking," I said.

She said, "Know what I was thinking?"

I gave her a nod to show I was listening.

"We should make a hit song and then live off the proceeds."

"How?" I said. "I used to play the accordion and I can't sing, and you sing badly and you don't play any instruments."

"I don't know either," she said. "But that Sinatra tune fed five generations."

I didn't know which Sinatra tune she had in mind, but I nodded just the same.

Right after that the phone rang; I picked up the receiver automatically and said, "Hello!"

My mother was calling. She said Josipa had disappeared— they'd been searching for her for days.

4

The first night I moved in as a first-year student to the Moša Pijade dorm on Victims of Fascism Square, I slept fitfully— I was woken by an unbearable, shrill squeal. Jolted awake, I jumped out of bed, pushed aside the heavy gray curtain, stared with curiosity out the window, and caught sight of the tail of the night tram as it slid slowly away and disappeared on its way to Borongaj.

One of my roommates—a student of politics who combined studying with lifting weights—asked me in the dark, "So, roomie, guess why it wails like that!"

"Why?"

"Because the tram is turning onto the Avenue of the Socialist Revolution," he said.

I offered no reaction at all, maybe he'd had been planted as a provocateur. Was he up to hoodwinking me into saying something against Yugoslavia, against socialism, so tomorrow I'd land in jail, bidding forever farewell to my career as a student?

I tried to fall back to sleep so I'd be ready for the next day's many obligations; I was the first student from the area where I grew up and I had big plans; this was still a time when not everybody went on to university—only the top students.

Whenever I returned to the village from the city, they'd call me "Student" and they uttered the word with respect, as if I were returning from a victorious revolution.

But the trams continued to disturb my sleep; whenever one turned down the Avenue of the Socialist Revolution, I'd find myself at the beginning again. During the day the piercing squeal was partially lost in the hustle and bustle of the city, but at night in the silence the squeal sounded chilling. It took me more than a month to acclimatize.

Along with the trams, in those early days, I was also disturbed and a little frightened by two men, oddballs, who came to sleep on the floor of our room, wrapped in blankets.

In conversations with them I realized they had no particular plans in life, that what mattered the most to them was getting a good night's sleep and scrounging tickets for the student cafeteria the next day.

"Flunked out," said the politics student. "But they used to be really great students."

One of the two guys, Branko from Šibenik, resolved to light a fire in the middle of the room on the parquet flooring one chilly night when the radiators were not working; we barely managed to dissuade him.

"What will you do if the dorm head comes by?" I asked them once.

"Into the wardrobe," said Branko in his cracking voice, reeking of booze. "It's illegal for the inspectors to check inside the wardrobes."

Otherwise, each year, Moša—our nickname for our dormitory—was the one that accommodated those first-year students who had too few points to qualify for the other dorms. After that freshman year they'd be off in a flash to the dormitories along the Sava River or the housing at Cvjetno Naselje, the Dr. Ante Starčević hall, or Laščina. The old stalwarts stayed behind at Moša, bolstered by the occasional newcomers, and the new, least fortunate freshmen. A dozen Black students were here from non-aligned nations, particularly Sudan. There were also quite a few Albanians and an attractive girl from India whose name was Sharma. Moša was decrepit, full of cockroaches, no student cafeteria, and there was once an epic chase down the hallways after a rat the size of a cat which had apparently come bounding out of a toilet bowl. Some twenty of us spent an entire night chasing after it with brooms and feet, and in the end it got away from us somewhere. After this unpleasant incident, the residents were terrified of sitting on the toilet until the rat slowly sank away into collective oblivion.

Moša was the only student dorm located right in the city center. There was a tram stop in front of the entrance and a fountain in the atrium, which Refik, a student from Novi Pazar, swam across for a few beers, despite the slime.

Across the street from the dorm, right by the round building we called the Mosque, there was another proudly spurting fountain and a different student, fully clothed, threw himself into that one on a dare. The police were promptly called and a race around the Mosque ensued, but the student, dripping wet, managed to slip into Lika, a bar nearby. He sipped a cognac while the cop, truncheon in hand, was still tensely searching the area around the Mosque.

The year I first moved into Moša there were rumors that the building would be sold, and that the days were numbered for this most venerable of all Zagreb's student dormitories which during the war had been an Ustasha prison. In some of the rooms there were still hooks on the walls that had been used to hang young communists by the feet; there were stories that rats had been forced into their rectums.

Every year the Union of Socialist Youth of Croatia published the magazine *Moša* at the dorm. Each issue—only one or two per year—made a point of telling and retelling the story of the person the dorm was named after, and his life and work as a revolutionary.

The first page was always the same—national hero Moša Pijade, known by his Partisan moniker Uncle Janko, translator of Marx's "Das Kapital" into the Serbian, author of the Foča regulations, organizer of the TANJUG news agency, and an exceptionally witty man. All this was supported by an anecdote or two.

I remembered one—Moša's friends teased him at a dinner by piling all their bones on his plate. Later they made fun of him, saying, "Look at Moša, such a puny man yet such a giant appetite." He fired back with, "People leave bones behind, but nothing is left behind by dogs."

*

Eli and I lay, slick with sweat and sperm, on the bed; a little later she nestled her head on my chest and fell asleep like that. Gently I moved her head over to the pillow, taking care not to wake her, wrapped a towel around my bare body and carefully opened the door which creaked like the doors in cheap horror films.

And besides, the room was very small, and the door opened inwards, only as much as the edges of the bed allowed, so it looked every time as if I were sneaking in like a thief.

In the hall I ran into my next-door roommate, Afrim, from Prishtina; he knew I was working through the student job service, and he had a sense of how bad my standing was at the university. A week before he'd said a little enigmatically that he had a terrific job lined up for me; that this was a job only for someone who could be trusted in life; I can't imagine where he got that from, that I was trustworthy. He stopped by my room several times, talked about his veterinary studies, about the Serbs he despised, and that was more or less it.

I asked him to tell me what sort of job he had in mind, but all he'd say was that I'd get the cash without having to lift so much as my little finger.

Now, I asked him about the job again, and he said that he still couldn't tell me anything about it, but he gave me a firm handshake and off he went up the stairs without another word.

Again I wondered, while I was in the shower, about what sort of job this could be. Nothing to do with drugs, I hoped; did he see my desperation as something that would drive me to that? Eli thought so. I'd conveyed every detail to her. She didn't like Afrim one bit; she thought he was cunning and underhanded.

*

"Eli," I said after emerging from under the gray dorm blanket. "I'm feeling a little peckish."

She said, "Me, too."

"Let's go to the Student Center cafeteria," I said.

"I don't feel like getting out of bed at all today," she said and glanced at my alarm clock—five o'clock in the afternoon.

"Do you have anything here in the room?" she asked.

"Just potatoes," I said.

She asked, "Could we make fries?"

"Sure," I said, bent over as if I were on a rowboat, and from under the bed I pulled out a white plastic bag half-full of potatoes. Some had already sprouted.

She selected a few, took the frying pan, cooking oil, and my hunting knife, and went off to the kitchenette down the hall to fry them up.

Not long after that I joined her, and when I walked in, she shot over to me and started kissing me. I lifted her up, she gaily wrapped her legs around my waist. I grabbed her by the bare bottom under her skirt, but the potatoes just then began to sizzle in the hot oil, so I set her down and watched how adeptly she flipped the fries.

She dumped another batch into the frying pan and again she hugged me hard; she hung with one arm around my neck and one leg pointing up at the ceiling; I made sure that nobody would come in because they could have seen her pussy.

When the frying pan began to sizzle again, she pranced back over to the stove.

"Why don't you go and make our bed and tidy things up a little in the room," she said over her shoulder.

I kissed her, went back to the room, made the bed, and smoothed the blanket over it. I took the miniature black-and-white television set, twenty centimeters square, off the shelf, plugged it in, pulled out the antenna, lay under the blanket, then set the television on my knees.

On the only working channel they were playing video spots, most of them by the bands we referred to as the New Romantics, with the grating sound of synthesizers that I had never been able to stomach. When Eli came back with the fried potatoes, I jumped up and put down the television, which began to crackle and hum so I switched it off.

"That contraption actually works," she jutted her chin toward the television.

"Of course."

"So, I thought it was a toy."

Once we'd eaten the fries, with me feeding her and her feeding me, I brought a bottle of water from the bathroom and put it down by the bed.

"Tonight, I'd really love to watch a good movie," she said.

"After the news there might be a movie on," I said.

When the newscast and the weather report had ended ... a series came on. The story took place in Zagreb during the

Second World War—young communists were preparing to assassinate a German officer. The officer went to the movies with his girlfriend and had no idea that they were shadowing him; they sat behind him. Tarzan yelled on the big screen and beat his breast, as if warning the officer of the danger.

"Did you know that this Tarzan came from around here?"

"No way," I said. "Johnny Weissmuller is American and guessing by his last name I assume his background is German," I said.

"He is German but he's from the Banat," said Eli, "and his real name is Hansi."

When the film ended, the German officer strolled with the girlfriend under an umbrella; the two young communists went on shadowing them closely and at one point their shadows, like shadows that nothing in this world can elude, slunk silently and simultaneously up to the officer and his girlfriend. They shot the officer in the head. The girl lay in a ditch and sobbed loudly while one of the young communists fired another bullet at the officer's head, just in case. They fled, but happened upon an Ustasha patrol, so they separated, and a chase ensued.

While the pounding thuds of boots on the wet Zagreb sidewalks were reverberating from the television, Eli said, "This is boring." I reached over and and turned it off and Eli began to tell me about her grandfather, a Partisan, who was killed at the battle of Sutjeska, then about her other grandfather, on her mother's side, whose apartment she was living in. I told her about my grandfather, that he'd been an Ustasha but he hadn't killed anybody; and that I'd introduce her to him one day—my grandfather on my mother's side died while my mother was just a little girl.

As a boy I used to like to poke around among old things; that's how I found my grandfather's leather briefcase in the attic, shoved under some floorboards, and wrapped in old rags. From one of its sections I took a yellowed sheet of newsprint from 1969, folded over several times, and on the creases the letters had faded and were less than legible in places. The article was about an event that happened during the Second World War in the Serbian Orthodox village of Crni Lug, with only a small patch of woods between them and us. Above the text was the title, THE MEMORIES OF A SURVIVOR.

Witness Milica Uzelac, who lives with her husband and two children in Ogulin, recalls through tears: the Ustashas informed us through some people that we should all come at noon to the middle of the village, where they'd conduct our religious conversion. Some of the people didn't want to and fled into the woods, while another group, including my parents, agreed to conversion to the Catholic faith, because word had got out that anyone who didn't comply would be sent to camps. The Ustashas arrived in the village a little after noon from the forest we call Plančica, and at their head rode an Ustasha on a white horse. Most of the Ustashas were from the neighboring village of Žliba ...

I went on reading, paying close attention, slowly following the words with my eyes. Then, again, I stopped, waited for my breathing to calm down, feeling that what I'd next read, each new syllable, would be even more painful, but my curiosity won out.

As I read on, chills began shivering from one verterbra to the next down my spine until I felt a strange turbulence in my stomach; then the salami sandwich I'd just eaten suddenly came up into my mouth. I gagged loudly a few more times.

My grandfather liked to tell stories about the Second World War; one of the most exciting was when an Allied plane crashed on our village, or in fact, right next to our village.

Granddad wasn't home then, but Granny told him all about it. The plane was shot down by the Ustashas in our village, but they didn't expect it to come down on the village; luckily it crashed right next to us. Granddad said the villagers took the plane apart faster than garage mechanics working on a Formula One. The fiercest scramble was for the steel fuel barrels that could be used to store grain or šljivovica. That's when I asked him, without directly mentioning what happened in Crni Lug, to tell me who the Ustasha was who rode a white horse. For a while Granddad was quiet, like always when he didn't know what to say.

Then he said, "Satan himself. He's to be blamed for everything."

✻

It was so wonderful kissing with Eli in bed that when she dozed off every now and then I'd pretend I just happened by chance to graze her with my elbow, and we'd start cuddling again. I didn't want to sleep through those wonderful moments.

For a few days the two of us hadn't left the student dorm and my room looked like a self-imposed solitary confinement cell for the two of us. I missed nothing, not the outside world, or music, or my pompadour, or sunlight. Eli was everything; I hugged her in a sweet stupor and wanted this to last forever.

✻

"What are you thinking about?" Eli asked me.

"About fucking you."

She said, "You're lying."

"I swear."

She smiled.

"And now?" she asked.

"I don't know," I said.

I drew her breast slowly out from under her tee shirt, put it in my mouth, felt how her nipple grew big in my mouth. She dropped to tongue my nipples, then my swollen prick, she tenderly drew the glans between her lips; her head between my legs went up, down, left, right, bounced about in my eyes.

When she was done, or rather when I was done and came

loudly in her mouth, I sighed deeply and said:

"Eli, you're really good at that."

Lying on her back and fishing one of my pubic hairs out of her mouth, she just smiled.

"You like giving head," I said.

"The best is giving head to a guy whose mother just died."

"You did that?" I said.

She smiled, then said, "Maybe."

"So, you're saying your junky's mother died?"

She looked over at me with my pubic hair between her fingers.

"Junky?"

"Your ex."

She went quiet, brushed off my pubic hair and ran her hand deeply through my hair.

"Hey, please, let's not talk about that."

We turned the television on again.

It was the same series, but now in reruns, partway through the episode we'd watched before. We decided to watch it to the end.

The Ustashas caught one of the young communists, the one who fired the last shot, and now they were cruelly torturing him; this time the scene was in the Ustasha prison, the very building where Eli and I were lying, happy and in love. I don't know whether Eli knew that this used to be an Ustasha prison; I chose not to tell her, better that she didn't know.

First, they lashed him with ox sinews. On the legs, head, genitals, but he wouldn't confess. They held his head underwater, but still he wouldn't confess. They took turns beating him and driving needles under his nails, but still he kept on stubbornly refusing. He wouldn't even tell them his name. Then with the last atom of strength he pulled free of one of his tormentors, threw himself through the window, and that's how he died and how the episode ended. After I turned the television off and put it on the floor, Eli, under the blanket, said, "If they tortured me like that, I'd give them all up."

"Excuse me?"

"I'd give them all up."

"How can you say that?" I said.

She said, "And you wouldn't?"

"I would not," I said.

"Hey, please, no bullshit."

"Come on, please, even if you'd give them up, at least say you wouldn't," I said, my voice slightly changed.

She said, "Unlike you, I'm being honest."

PART TWO

PART TWO

5

At first my right ear began aching at night, I figured it would pass, but then it began hurting even more. The pain kept me from sleeping even for a minute. I suffered with this for three nights in a row, and Eli kept urging me to see the doctor at the Student Health Service.

I wasn't eager to go. I'm scared of hospitals and any place that resembles a hospital. Compelled by the pain I finally caved in and somehow managed to get myself there. It was only a few steps away; the health service was in a wing attached to my dormitory.

When my turn finally came—I waited from 8 a.m. to noon—the young doctor shone a light in my ear and said my ear was in fine shape.

That evening the ear ached less, by morning it had stopped aching altogether, but the next day my throat began to hurt. Actually, it's that something was scratchy in there, then little by little my throat began to tighten, as if there were a lump in it, a lump wrapped in prickles. At first I thought I'd caught a cold, and what mattered most was that my ear wasn't aching any more. I drank teas; but not only did the throat thing not pass—it got worse, so there were times when I felt as if my heart had climbed up into my throat, where it was throbbing and sure to choke me.

After a few days of anguish, I could no longer swallow properly (it would take me half an hour to eat a mouthful of sandwich), food kept lodging in my throat, and I began to panic that my gullet would become so constricted that I'd no longer be able to swallow a thing. At those moments of panic, especially when I was trying to fall asleep, I distracted myself by thinking about something else—films, books, Eli's boobs. Over and over I'd say, "This will pass, this will pass."

I hadn't told Eli anything about the thing with my throat. But after a few days I began to feel as if I were swinging on a tightening noose, so I told her everything. She immediately said I should see a psychiatrist.

"Why a psychiatrist?" I said. "Why not an ordinary doctor?"

"First you go to your ordinary doctor for the referral."

Then she said, by way of consolation, "This is perfectly normal, I've been to a psychiatrist plenty of times."

The next day I took the referral from the young doctor and went up to the next floor to see the psychiatrist. I had never talked with a psychiatrist in my life, though my mother, when she was really furious at me, often said that one of these days I'd definitely end up in a madhouse. I felt extremely uncomfortable there among the people who were waiting by the door to the office—each gazing at a point of their own. I stared out the window.

After two hours my turn came; someone inside called

my name, I slipped in quickly, as if I didn't want my first and last name to escape, to be exposed. The psychiatrist was a woman, not a man; she might have been about fifty. She was sitting in a deep armchair. She gestured for me to sit on the chair across from her, while in the other hand she held her phone and was telling someone in a calm voice, "Young man, if you feel you're losing your mind, then, I assure you, you will not. People who feel they're losing their mind never do."

Her words already offered me a modicum of comfort.

The psychiatrist hung up, picked up the referral, looked at it, then looked over at me, and her gaze lingered on my leather jacket.

"How much does a jacket like that cost?" she asked.
"200 Deutschmarks."

"You bought it here?"

"At a flea market in Germany a few years ago."

"Are there any like that around here?" she asked.

"There are, but not as nice as this one," I said. "If you fall off a motorcycle when you're wearing this, you won't get all smashed up."

"You drove here on a motorcycle?" she asked.

"No," I said. "I don't have a bike."

Drawing the curtain behind her, she said, "My son wants a jacket like that, so I've been having a look around."

I settled more comfortably in the chair and unbuttoned the jacket; she looked me in the eyes and said, "So, talk!"

"About what?"

"About why you're here," she smiled.

I took a deep breath, and started to tell her about my ear, my throat . . .

"What are you most afraid of in life?" she interrupted me. "Tell me quickly."

"Snakes," I said.

"What else?"

"Death."

"Do you have a big exam coming up or something important you're expecting soon?" she asked.

"I'll be a father," I said.

"Ah, congratulations!" she said. "Wonderful news."

Then she told me I should tell her how I was feeling as an expectant father.

I didn't know what to say, then I told her I hadn't yet completed my studies, I was broke, but I loved my girlfriend and wanted to have a child with her. I wasn't entirely certain of this last point. I told her that, too.

"Hardly surprising that you're not certain," she said. "Certainty is the greatest of human failings and those who are overly sure of themselves are often very dangerous people. Hitler was sure of himself, and you know what he did."

I nodded and from time to time I looked down at her black ballet flats; she kept shuffling them off and then slipping them back on, as if pumping a Singer sewing machine. This was also how she spoke, in a measured tone, rhythmically: ticka-tocka, ticka-tocka.

"What I meant to say is that your fear has shown up in your throat," she said. "Fear for the future. You're still young, you have no job, you have yet to graduate, you're carrying too great a burden, like a young fruit tree when its branches bend under the weight, but you'll succeed, you're tough, I can see that."

She prescribed me pills and said I should take them regularly, three times a day, and come back for a follow-up. She stood, shook my hand, saw me to the door.

I raced out of the waiting room so nobody I knew would spot me there, dashed down the well-worn stairs, and over the road to the nearest pharmacy.

I bought the pills, the size of small grains, took one and hopped onto a tram headed for Republic Square. I got off at the stop before the square because I felt as if I'd start gagging right there on the tram; though I didn't know how I'd retch, what with my numb jaw. I walked along Jurišićeva Street like a robot with my screws loose; my head loose, my gaze fixed. I still had the strength to reach into my pocket, grab the box of pills and toss it into the first trash can.

Then step into the nearest entryway, sit there in the dark, and slap myself hard on the head to make my damned head finally start working.

I am standing by a window for a while; outside the wind is stripping the last leaves from the trees. The gusts are building in force, but I seem to be in the middle of a vortex. I feel as if I'm moving farther from myself, like a boat drifting off from the shore, heading out toward looming, black waves.

Eli was making dinner, she was skipping around the

kitchen, she'd never been happier, and when she was happy she wanted everyone around her to be happy—she kept coming over to me to ask whether I was OK. I didn't want to spoil her mood so I kept quiet and nodded that I was fine, but never in my life had I been worse.

To be fair, I was no longer having the difficulties with my throat, but recently the thing with pressure in my chest that used to trouble me was starting up again. Now it was so powerful, at times, that I felt as if my ribs might pop out from their joints.

Mostly I'm having trouble breathing, for whole days I'm a lot like a fish gasping for air. The nights are the worst, it is strangling me, and I feel, if I succumb to sleep, I'd die.

In the morning, when I wake up—still alive after all—the pressure in my chest is gone for a full five minutes, but then it reappears.

I went to lie down, squinted in the dark, my eyes crumbled into dust and the dust choked me, and that's the way this went every evening.

I got up and told Eli, who'd lain down beside me and was reading a book, that I was going out for a walk; I ran around the building late at night, tried to snatch this thing out of me, scrabbling at my chest with my hands.

At one point I screamed so loudly in anguish that I reminded myself of that figure in Munch's "The Scream". Someone who was passing by ran into a well-lit place and began calling in panic for help; I, myself, was on the verge of calling for help with all my strength.

After a few days, Eli suggested a healer she'd heard about.

I went to see the man at his family home where he lived in the part of town called Trešnjevka. The yard was crowded with people. I hadn't felt this much negative energy in one place in a long time, but, I figured, that's to be expected.

When my turn came, as I shouldered my way through the crowd, a man with bristle-stiff hair asked me to strip to the waist. He palpated my chest and said that my diaphragm was constricting, and this was the root of the problem; he also said that people who had problems with their diaphragm hadn't been loved in childhood. He moved around me in a circle and with palms extended he sliced the air; he did this for about fifteen minutes. Then he rested his hand on my chest. That felt nice. I felt his hand soothe me, as if I were about to drop off to sleep.

I paid and left but felt no better. I went a few more times to him for treatments and then gave up.

I got up with a metallic taste in my mouth, as if I'd had been sucking on a bullet all night. I washed with cold water, for a long time watching it meander and run down the sides of the washbasin into the drain.

I closed the tap tightly and went to the window—Eli was still sleeping, it was a rain-drenched Sunday, long and boring, the worst day of the week; even, perhaps, of my entire shitty life.

I gasped for air and stared feverishly out the window—at black clouds, rundown buildings, people under umbrellas who walked and looked like flat-headed nails. I'd have loved not to be compelled to look at that, I'd have loved not having to look at anything.

In the double windowpane I caught sight of my own sagging shoulders, tousled hair, the striped pajamas that Eli's grandfather had worn. They were baggy on me.

I picked up the remote control and clicked: on one channel Tom was chasing Jerry with an axe, but Jerry was saved, with his rapid mousy steps, by darting last minute into his lair in the wall, a lair I'd longed for as a boy when my father beat me for no reason.

One cold winter evening I was watching Tom and Jerry in secret. I was so glued to what was happening on the screen that I let Father creep up behind me; I'd been keeping an eye out for him through the window, poised to turn off the television in time, but Tom and Jerry captivated me. Father heard the television when he was at the door, too late for me to turn it off. All we were allowed to watch was the weather report—one of his rules. For instance, whenever I reached into the fridge, I had to think first about what I'd take and then quickly open it and grab what I was after because he said that if warm air got in there it would damage the fridge and ruin it.

I froze. Father opened the door and stood in the doorway, stomping the snow off his boots as if running in place, and I felt as if he were running after me.

I sat there, rigid, expecting him to grab me from behind by the ears, twist them, and then hoist me into the air by them, as he was wont to do. This time he pulled up his chair, and, smelling of alcohol, he sat down next to me in silence. I stared at the screen and was expecting, any minute, a slap.

When the cartoon ended and nothing happened, I stood, bewildered, switched the television off and chose the farthest chair, by the stove, fearful that a slap might still be in the offing: he looked at me and swayed, drunkenly, on the chair.

He told me, mumbling, that a half hour before down at the tavern they'd caught a mouse, much like the one on television, when it came leaping out of the cash register.

"Ten of us chased it till we caught it," he said, staring off through the wall, his words trapped behind his big teeth.

He told me how our neighbor Marko was the first to spot it in the cash register, and then, again, he said they all ran around after it for ages, chasing it under the tables and chairs.

He lifted his head a little, looked over at me, and said, "I, I was the one who caught it."

I recognized him in these words, his need to boast, which I inherited from him. I bit my tongue as he spoke, looking out at the heavy snow that was falling, and then finally I took a breath and asked, "So what did you do with the mouse?"

With pity in his voice, he said, "I felt bad for it, so I threw it into the wood stove."

I was strolling along Ilica, varying my pace, window-shopping, and as if through fog I heard someone from the throng of passersby calling me by name. I had forgotten what my given name sounded like. I turned and saw Zdravko, my best friend from elementary school. He was standing, built like an athlete, in a suit and tie, with his pregnant wife and two children, beckoning me over.

When I joined him, his two children stared at me as if I were a monster and burst into tears; if I'd had my pompadour, I'd have thought the hairdo was to blame. Zdravko hugged me warmly, introduced me to his wife, who I was meeting for the first time, and told her to quiet the children.

"So what are you up to?" he said.

"Walking along Ilica," I joked.

He clapped me on the shoulder.

"We're on our way to a nearby pastry shop, why don't you come along?" he said.

I hesitated, but he had already taken me firmly by the arm and with resolute stride was steering me. We sat at a low table, Zdravko asked me what I'd have to eat and drink, and I asked for a Zagreb kremšnita and a Coke.

"Still drinking Coke?" he laughed.

"Oh, not me," I said.

"Well, I haven't had a Pepsi in years," he said. "I could now," he said.

He asked for a Pepsi, but they didn't offer it, so he ordered a piece of apple pie and a Coke. Then in front of the waiter he asked his wife and children what they'd like; after that he turned to me again, and again he asked, "So, what are you up to?"

"Not much," I said.

"I haven't seen you in ages," he flashed me that characteristic, superior grin of his.

Zdravko was my next-door neighbor until I was five, but his father worked in Germany and built them a house in town, so they moved there. Zdravko was considered the strongest boy at school, and he played the best soccer; if a boy happened to out-dribble him, Zdravko would catch up and simply slap the boy across the face.

He was two years older than me, but he'd had to repeat two grades, so we were together for our last two years of elementary school.

I was proud to hang out with him and have him as my best friend. He often took me along when he hung out with girls; he'd insult me in front of them, laugh at me, that was how he tried to impress them, but this didn't bother me at all, I cared much more about being his friend.

I often did his homework for him and made drawings for him for his art portfolio. Our theme was once "Darkness on Pathways of Light." I didn't know what to draw for myself or for him, so I gave him back his sheet of paper with nothing on it. He kicked me in the ass and told me to draw something, anything.

Then I colored both our sheets of paper all black and drew little yellow stars on them, except there were more little stars on his and a stag, so our drawings wouldn't look too much alike; his drawing was marked as excellent with a grade of five, and mine as very good, with a four.

Today he is one of the richest people in town, he runs a butcher shop, an abattoir, and two big trucks.

"I'm planning a farm, and since you are one of the rare people with schooling where we're from, you might give some thought to moving back. We need educated people there," he said in a serious voice.

Then, after he sent his wife and children off for a walk, he told me softly that he'd heard there were preparations underway for the first democratic elections, and that Croatia would soon be free and as prosperous as Switzerland.

"Paradise awaits us," he whispered. "All we need to do is get rid of those communists."

＊

Eli was a skillful driver; she sped, passed, honked; I was indifferent, I didn't even care if we crashed.

As we were leaving Zagreb, she took out a TDK cassette and inserted it into the tape deck.
At the first beats of the melody, she began shaking her head and pounding the rhythm on the steering wheel with her hand.

The voice was Leonard Cohen's and the song, "You Know I Am." About a woman to bear and kill his children.

I said, "Come on, turn that off."

Singing, she asked, "But why?"

"Because I find it fucking depressing."

She listened a little longer and then turned it off.

We raced along the Zagreb–Karlovac highway, the

rain stopped, clouds scudded across the sky. Eli drove fast, sometimes she'd surge by cars so it looked as if they were standing still in comparison.

I never would have imagined that this red Renault 4 could go so fast, and it shuddered as if at any moment it was about to fall apart. The shuddering that shook my body reminded me of the shuddering of a rocket seconds before it launches into outer space. Something suddenly whisked by us, behind us, I couldn't see it properly, as if it were a bird or the shadow of a bird. I looked over at Eli. Her gaze was just then returning from the rear-view mirror. She slowed down a little.

"What happened?" I asked.

"Plastic," she said.

"What plastic?"

"Came off the door," she said.

After a moment I said, "Should we go back for it?"

"Why go back?"

"Somebody might crash into the plastic," I said.

"No need," she said. "What could possibly happen?"

"I don't know," I said, worried.

"I can't just stop the car and turn back."

"You could have pulled over to the side of the road, and one of us could have gone back and removed the plastic."

" Who knows where it flew off to? Maybe it's not even on the road."

"Maybe it is, maybe it isn't," I said.

"Fuck it now," she said and shook her head as if she didn't know what to do next. "The cars will deal with it."

"What if they don't deal with it, what if it deals with

them, and besides the highway is wet."

"But what if a motorist hits it and loses control," I said. Eli was still quiet, then she pulled over at the first wayside tavern to ask for the phone.

I went in with her, the tavern was empty, full of stifling silence. The only waitress was by the bar, her face caked with a thick layer of makeup.

Taxidermied animals had been mounted on the wall; they watched us with marbles instead of eyes, as if they planned to enchant us with their gaze.

The waitress gave her the phone; Eli called the local authority for the highway.

"Plastic," she said.

"A piece of plastic fell off," she repeated.

Then she listened, explained, nodded, and returned the phone to the waitress.

"How much do I owe you?" she asked.

"Nothing," said the waitress.

We thanked her in unison and left.

"What did they say?" I asked as we walked.

"Nothing, they think I'm crazy."

"What matters is that we reported it," I said.

We sat in the car and continued along the winding road.

"I feel as if I fled from the scene of an accident," said Eli, mastering the many bends on the road.

"Nothing will happen," I said.

"Of course it won't, but you filled me with paranoia."

"Now it's my fault."

She didn't say another word. For another fifty kilometers

or so she drove on in silence. Just before we entered the town, which was nestled in a hollow, we passed a woman who was carrying a basket on her head, balanced on a head ring, then we went by two cows standing, blithely, mid-road. She sped up, then took her foot off the gas, taking care that the other cows, grazing by the roadside, didn't saunter out in front of the car.

She drove on slowly, and I saw the movie theater I used to go to, my elementary school, the store on the ground floor of a rundown house where the fat storekeeper made sandwiches for me from tirolska salama; we drove by, I looked, closed my eyes, kept the image in my eyes, then looked again.

"Where should we go first, the police or the hospital?" asked Eli.

"The police," I said.

"Where's the station?"

"You'll have to back up," I said.

I showed her the squarish building over which tall, powerful trees were craning their necks, and she drove me up to it and turned off the engine.

I kissed her, checked what I looked like in the window of another car, smoothed my hair back. Recently this was how I'd been doing my hair; I couldn't remember the last time I'd worked up a pompadour.

I walked the few steps over to the police station, the sand crunching under my boots. I had been here only once—when I was in my final year of elementary school; I was chosen as one of the three best students who had the honor of congratulating the police for Police Day.

I wiped my shoes on the rag by the door, knocked, and a mustachioed policeman opened it. His name was Milan. I greeted him and said why I'd come. He looked me up and down, nodded, picked up the phone and said, "Chief, sir?"

The chief was Boba's father.

Milan offered me a chair, asked what the Zagreb weather was like, I told him rainy, and he said they'd also had rain but now it had stopped.

Boba's father soon appeared, tall, craggy, a thin mustache under his nose, looking like a Hollywood B-lister. He walked with a remarkable spring in his step and his cap with the shiny red five-pointed star was tilted back on his head. He shook my hand, sat at his desk, and Milan sat on a bench behind me.

"Do you know why we called you?" asked Boba's father.

"I do," I answered.

"What can you tell us?"

"Nothing," I said.

"When was the last time you saw her?" he said and scribbled something in his notebook.

"My cousin Slavo roasted a hare at his place, and that's where I saw her last."

"Did you notice Slavo eyeing her strangely?"

"He was eyeing her strangely the whole time because he was in love with her," I said.

Boba's father kept watching me with those hawk-like eyes of his; he had the gaze of a person who won't miss a thing in the room. He was also handy with the truncheon. He liked beating people. I heard from a man that Boba's father once said, "The pain from the beating has to kill the desire to sing Ustasha songs."

"That will be all," said Boba's father. "If there's anything else we need, we'll be in touch."

I got up and asked him about Boba.

"She's in Belgrade, she earned her medical degree and now she's waiting for her residency," he said.

"Please give her my regards," I said.

He put a cigarette in his mouth, nodded, flicked the lighter and lit it. I doubted he'd convey my regards.

I went to the Renault. Eli was staring out the window.

"How did it go?"

"Fine."

She asked, "To your house first or the hospital?"

"Let's go see Father on our way back. Mama might have something to send him."

*

Eli parked out by the road because the horse cart was blocking the path to my house.

I took her by the hand and brought her to the house by a different path, over the meadow.

Eli liked the wildness of it, walking through grass, she breathed in the bracing air, then swooned, shrieked, slipped and nearly fell. She collected herself, took me by the arm, and said, "Such stunning nature."

Mama kissed Eli, she'd already met her once in Zagreb, and she knew Eli was pregnant. Father still hadn't met Eli, but Mama told him I was going to be a father; I don't know how he reacted; probably not at all.

Mama quickly fixed us some food, and as we were eating, she began talking again about the time a few days before, when Father was working in the yard on a gate for the pigsty and gashed his leg with his axe.

"Blood came gushing out like from a tap," she said.

Marko the neighbor soon turned up to say hello. Then came Miško the Roma. One of his young sons was with him, and he whacked the boy for no reason so the kid began to whimper, and then he kicked him in the butt and sent him out. Mama took a piece of candy from the cupboard and brought it out to him, and the boy quieted down outside. Then Mijo, Josipa's father, came and said hi; he asked me in a low voice whether the police had any information.

"They didn't say a thing," I said. "They spent about ten minutes asking me questions, whether I know anything, but I know less than you do."

Mijo, Marko and Miško stood there in silence for a while, waiting for me to say more, then they said their goodbyes and left.

Mama asked me whether I'd seen Slavo.

"Where would I have seen him?" I said. "I only just got here."

"I mean there at the station," she quieted a cough with her hand.

I looked at her and knit my eyebrows, while dipping bread in the chicken gravy.

She said, "He has been held at the police station for five

days now. He's their suspect, he bought her a ring, but she spurned him. I think he snapped, and then he took her, dead, up to the pit," she said.

"Hey, please, I'm eating," I said with a grimace, while Eli ate and looked out the window.

Mama went to the stove, bent over, pushed in more logs.

"Some people saw him at the station," she said and poked around among the embers with her iron poker. "That he was all black and blue, they're beating him, and he, the fool, won't admit to what he's done."

Eli went on listening and eating slowly. I tried to serve her a little more, but she showed me with a gesture that she wouldn't want more.

"How are you faring?" Mama suddenly asked her.

"Well, thank you," said Eli, startled.

"Morning sickness?" asked Mama.

"A little," said Eli.

After half an hour Mama packed underwear for Father, and she tucked 100 Deutschmarks in my pocket, taking care that nobody, not even Eli, could see, and in a thin voice she said, "It's from the milk—even your dad doesn't know about it."

A little later we said goodbye to Mama, sat in the car and drove into town. Then I remembered I'd forgotten to take some of my own shirts and T-shirts, but I wasn't eager to go back. When we arrived at the intersection and when Eli asked me where the hospital was, I told her to drive straight on. On she drove, and then she said, "Wait, but this is the road out of town . . ."

"Just drive," I said.

"And your dad?" she asked.

"Not right now."

"You sure are . . ."

I barked, "Is he your father or mine?"

"Fine," she said, stepping on the gas. "Cool it."

I went with Eli to a department store have a look at things for the child; we still didn't know whether it was a boy or a girl, though Eli said she had a feeling it was a boy. We vanished into the whirligig of revolving glass doors and wandered around the children's department.

She kept fingering items of children's clothing, stretching them, asking the sales assistant questions, and like a puppy I walked along behind her and nodded, even when she wasn't asking me anything.

We also went to the toy department. Eli had a look at plastic blocks.

"When I was little, I was very destructive, a friend would build something with blocks and I'd knock it right down," she laughed.

The next day I went with her to see a gynecologist. For a time we sat, hugging, on red plastic chairs; there was another pregnant woman with a little boy in the waiting room. After a few minutes the nurse called Eli; I stood up to stretch my legs and walked around the waiting room.

The little boy began to suck his thumb, and the pregnant woman told him, "If you suck your thumb, you'll grow a tail."

I went out onto the grimy street, kicked a rock around, and waited for Eli. When we returned home, Eli dropped onto the bed, exhausted, still in her lace-up boots.

"Do you even realize we're having a child?"

"I do," I said, in a fog.

"What do you think, what sort of mother will I be?" she asked.

"Terrific," I said, just so she wouldn't ask me anything more about that.

Then she began to cry.

I went over to her, worried.

"What's wrong?"

"I remembered a boy," she said.

"Who?"

"He was with me in elementary school, and then when we were in our final year he threw himself under a train."

Now she cried even harder, and in a soft voice I urged her to stop.

"He was poor, his apartment was filthy, he once invited us to his birthday party, and nobody went, not even me, there, that's why I'm crying," she began to sob.

"Hey, calm down," I said. "Never, even once, did I have a birthday party."

"Why was I like that?" she wailed. "Why?"

✻

First I stood on one leg for a while, then on the other, and looked out the window; it had been half an hour since fitfulness had taken hold of my legs; my whole body was shivering as if I had a bad fever. My forehead was clammy, but just in case, I took my thermometer, tucked it under my arm, and the mercury barely crept above thirty-six degrees.

Eli had already gone to the bedroom and had probably fallen asleep, reading. I paced around the kitchen, watched television, gnawed at my nails, tried to calm down—then I opened the window, stuck my head out, tried to breathe.

After a few minutes I began to feel as if my head, sticking that way out of the window, were separate from my body, from the whole world. Then, with trembling hand, I shut the window behind me.

Later it occurred to me that in the evening perhaps I could work on those bicycles of hers in the cellar. Though Eli should not be riding hers and I wouldn't be needing one, the work would help get me through yet another damned night. I needed to fiddle with something; it would be soothing. And besides Eli would be glad that I'd fixed the bikes; she'd asked me to work on them six months earlier.

In the hallway I found the cardboard box with tools— pliers and a screwdriver—and taking the keys to the cellar and storage unit, off I went. I descended quickly into the dark and dank, chilly cellar, groped for the light switch in the dark and clicked it on, but the lightbulb was so cloudy and wan that it lit only itself.

Making my way gingerly, I traversed thick slabs of darkness; our storage unit was the last one. I unlocked it, went in, and switched on the fixture that spilled light from the dusty bulb into every corner of the longish space.

The walls were layered with damp and spiderwebs, the air was stagnant, heavy, but I was so far gone, such a wilted flower that I didn't breathe, shivering more than the worst possible junky going cold turkey.

There at the back of the storage unit, the darkest part, or maybe from one of the other units, came twitchy sounds, as if someone were playing on a comb; the sound kept coming, then fading. I ventured slowly from the light into the gloom, stepping over a heap of discarded boards, taking care not to trip over them and fall.

The bicycles were right there beyond the boards. When I came closer, something suddenly leaped out; I jumped back and then slowly, step-by-step, crept up to the bikes. I took a closer look; Eli's bike seat was all chewed up—it was hollowed out with a mouse nest; the baby mice still hadn't opened their eyes. The mother must have been the one leaping from the nest.

I stood with one side of my face in the dark; for a time I looked at them quietly, how they were milling around in the hollowed-out seat like the gears in a clock. Then I took a step back, chose a board, lifted it over my head and began whacking. The mice squealed, the bicycles rattled, blood splattered over the walls, the sounds mingled and bounced off the walls, I kept whacking, I didn't stop, and the board I was swinging pulled me in every direction around the unit.

When I finished, and had probably smashed everything, I flung the board down, went outside and looked, drained, up at the sky; the stars were shining, and those pulsing stars looked like the eyes on the hiding mice.

✳

That evening I felt as if I truly wouldn't make it; I couldn't breathe and there were a few times when I came very close to calling an ambulance. But instead of running to the phone I ran to the bathroom and began puking; I knelt in front of the toilet bowl and retched; I had nothing left in me to vomit; my tears of misery were all that dripped down into the toilet bowl.

At one moment I struggled to my feet and went to the fridge, pulled out a bottle of šljivovica, downed half of it. Now that was better.

I went back to bed next to Eli and greeted the next morning sitting up, a pillow behind my back, still struggling to breathe.

My head throbbed inside my eye, I felt a cough scratching inside my chest. But if I coughed, I felt as if my brain would come squirting out through my eye socket, though I couldn't tell which eye—left or right.

I decided to take the first bus to see a priest Eli had mentioned a few days before. Through her mother she got the address—while I stood there she told her mother that she was asking for a friend, and she gave me the money for the ticket. Then she kissed me, wrapped me in a hug for a long time and said, "I love you," in my ear.

✳

I arrived in Split by bus and asked at the information counter about the place where I was going, then took a city bus to Omiš. I bought the ticket from the driver and went to sit at the back; as I rode along I watched the sea foaming, then caught myself picking my teeth with the ticket.

As I stared out at the sea, I began to feel as if everything interesting in my life had already happened and it would be better if I were old and dead. Then I started paying attention to the signs along the road and soon I got off.

I wanted to ask someone where the church was. I couldn't see it. I was standing below gray cliffs, and a dozen houses were packed close together at their foot. The sea behind me was madly pounding the shore so I had to step back to keep my feet from getting splashed.

I looked around for the church and my gaze met the road; I noticed a flattened glove and immediately took this as a sign, a finger of fate; and one finger of the glove was, indeed, pointing toward those houses.

I started up the macadam road, then I noticed that one of the buildings near the top of the cliffs was, in fact, both a house and a church; a cross was carved into the façade. I walked along, met nobody, saw nobody, arrived at the house–church that was tucked in between the rocks and another house, knocked at the door behind which I could hear the droning of an organ. I waited a little longer, eyeing the well-tended garden, which looked as if it were straight from a tourist brochure, young branches trained onto poles on which beans were drying. The door was opened by a broad-shouldered, dark-complexioned man with jutting nostrils.

He let me pass by without a word and then closed the door behind us; he was wearing a T-shirt and jeans and wore scruffy espadrilles. He took me down a dark hallway, paved in black-and-white tiles, to a sunlit room; a waterfall of light fell on the altar through a glass portion of the roof.

In a low voice the man told me to wait, and then he disappeared behind the altar. When he reappeared, he was wearing the white robes of a priest.

I remained silent, not knowing what I was supposed to be saying to him; when I finally started to speak, he pointed to his mouth that I shouldn't.

He returned behind the altar and this time brought out a smallish metal cross which he asked me to kiss. I would have kissed his ass if only he could help me; I kissed the cross and he drew several unfamiliar signs with it around my head. He passed the cross over my body, head to heel, like the police at the airport do with their wands.

When he stopped, he told me to kneel at the altar, close my eyes and say the "Our Father" out loud; I knelt below the dense motionless light, began to pray, fumbled, and kept going back to the beginning, "Our Father, who art in heaven, hallowed be thy name, thy kingdom come . . . Our Father, who art . . ."

"Keep going, Satan is holding you back," he said from behind.

After a while I was able to pray, and felt as if the whole afternoon had passed, then opened my eyes and looked around. The priest wasn't there. I stopped praying, was about to get up, drew one leg forward so I looked as if I were poised in a starting half-crouch, about to lope off at any moment.

Then I heard a sound behind me; he popped out like a white billiard ball from a pocket; in his hands he was holding the pole I'd seen used for drying the beans. He brandished it in my direction, I automatically raised both hands to protect my head, but the pole bashed straight through my hands and struck me right on the head. Then another blow and yet another which knocked me to the stone floor. I groaned, tried to say something, but the blows rained down on me, on my arms, legs, head, so I hunched up and guarded my head with my arms.

When the blows finally ended and I was sure I was dead, the priest came over, lifted me up, gave me water; as if I'd been wounded in the field of battle. Then he said, "Son, now you're freed."

I got up, still quite dazed, touching my head: no blood. That's how the police do it where I'm from. They beat you but there is never anything to show for it.

The priest let me lean on him and saw me out without a word. He said goodbye with the firm squeeze of a hand.

I could barely totter down the path, walking as if balancing on a ball, everything around me feeling distant, then veering closer; I kept having to lean on things, feeling like a not-quite-squashed bug. That must be how I was walking, too. Somehow, I dragged myself to the water's edge, sat on the first rock, moistened my dried, chapped lips with my tongue, and when the bus came, I could barely tear my gaze away from the sea; I thought I had become completely unhinged.

*

It is five days since I went to see that priest; the pains from the bean pole are over, sure. I can still feel them a little, especially now as I'm reclining and fidgeting on the seat of this uncomfortable train. But what's going on in my head is just the same as it was before I went to see the priest; I'm not fully alive nor am I fully dead.

I opened my eyes, smelled smoke; then from my reclining position I propped myself up on my elbow, turned and on the seat across from me I saw an old man. He had unnaturally green eyes; in the corner of his tightly pressed lips there was a cigarette burning down.

"Where are we?" I managed to ask and looked through the window at the villages, some densely packed, others scattered.

The old man didn't say a word, in his mouth he adroitly maneuvered his cigarette to the other corner of his lips and inhaled another hit; I thought maybe he was a deaf mute. The train traversed a mountainous gorge, the sun shone through the thick forest. I took a comb from my back pocket and combed my hair, and then ran my hand over it once more.

"Where are you going?" asked the old man suddenly, and those strange eyes of his reflected all the things in the compartment.

I told him the name of the town.

He nodded and inhaled another hit of smoke, as if by inhaling he was speeding the train along.

Again I looked out the window, the forest had grown all the way to the edge of the view. A few minutes later, at the next station, he went out into the corridor; I tried to help him with his bag, but he gestured with his free hand that he could manage; with that same gesture he bid me goodbye.

I heard a garbled, yodel-like sound—and looked out. Because of the singing and Serbian flags, I thought the people were there for a wedding or a soccer game.

Then, for the first time, I saw a genuine Chetnik—as if straight out of the war movie "The Battle of Neretva." He was brandishing a Serbian flag on a long pole and singing "Shine on, oh bright Kosovo sun / We will not relinquish you, land of Dušan." The crowd around him—some waving pictures of Slobodan Milošević high above their heads—went on singing even more loudly, "Without bloodshed we won't let you go / Oh, our beloved land of heroes." Everyone looked as if they were arguing about something with the iron monster that was stopped there at the station.

Then, finally, the train began to move. The sun soon helped me forget the spectacle of the Chetnik.

We trundled slowly along, jolting as if we were riding in a cart on iron wheels. The sun traveled slowly from window to window.

When the train finally rolled into the station where I was getting off, across the road I spotted Slavo's dark blue Zastava 101 that Mama had told me about—he'd bought it the week before.

Slavo was smoking, standing beneath a wide-branching tree; my mother was sitting motionless in the car. She'd called the night before to say she'd like me to come home so we could go together to visit my sister; it was my nephew's third birthday.

I had the feeling that a change of scenery might do me good, and besides she'd probably give me some money, but my one condition was that I wouldn't come to the house because I didn't have the energy for an encounter with my father.

I left the train. A breeze was blowing, it envigorated me. I went over to Slavo, we shook hands, he grasped mine firmly, and clapped me on the back.

With his eyes he gestured proudly at the car parked in the deep shade. Mama got out; we shook hands.

"Do you want to sit in the front or the back," she asked me.

"I don't care." I took the seat next to Slavo.

Angrily he propped up the hood of the car and puttered with something because it wouldn't start and Mama slipped me a 100-Deutschmark bill from the back seat, tucking it into my pocket.

"When you get there, give this to the boy in front of everybody," she said. "I haven't got any for you right now."

Slavo got back into the car and started it up; we let a horse-drawn cart go first and then off we went.

My sister lives on the edge of town. A big house, three floors with outbuildings, two vehicles, a roomy garage—her husband is a car mechanic, one of the most respected where I'm from; his hands are always black and greasy.

Slavo stepped on the gas and lurched into the curves, his tires screeching, as if he were out to punish his car because it hadn't wanted to start.

"What's up in the village?" I asked.

"Nothing much," said Slavo.

"Any word about Josipa?" I asked.

Mama said, "It's like the ground swallowed her whole." Slavo trod even more fiercely on the gas, passing a trailer truck.

"Now there's talk," said my mother, "that she was consorting with Granddad for years."

"Whose granddad?" I looked back at her.

"Ours, the deceased, he should be ashamed of himself up there in heaven," she shook her head and retied the knot on her kerchief.

"Oh, that's not true," said Slavo.

"That's what they're saying," said Mama. "And the two of them did tend the cattle together up there in the forest."

"So what?" said Slavo. "So what? Somebody would have noticed this a long time ago, not now."

As they talked, I was staring wordlessly out the window in shock, at some lit-up letters.

"They're saying she was pregnant," said Mama.

"Pregnant with whom?" I winced.

"With our granddad, God forgive him," she crossed herself.

"Oh, that's not true," said Slavo.

"How do you know, Slavo?" she said. "Like you're Mr. Expert all of a sudden."

"Come on, Mama," I said. "Stop making stuff up."

"That's what people around here are saying," she said.

"And where there's smoke, I say there's bound to be fire."

"They're so full of shit," said Slavo and spun the steering wheel.

"I'm telling you, Slavo my boy, there's something to this," she said. "I'm just sorry they locked you up, poor child, and beat you, when you were as innocent as the day is long. Instead of looking for the real murderer."

"Fuck their Chetnik mothers," said Slavo.

"Here's what I think," Mama said in hushed tones as if she were afraid someone might hear. "When her daddy figured out she was pregnant with our granddad, God forgive him, he killed her for the shame of it, dragged her up to the pit and threw her in. That's what I said to Dad and he, too, thinks the same. That the poor thing is up there in the pit."

"Stop it, Mama!" I shouted. "Stop making stuff up!"

When we got there, my sister saw us from the window. She came racing down the stairs and opened the red gate with its wrought-iron flowers.

My brother-in-law was at the grill, and this must have been the first time I'd ever seen him when his hands weren't greasy and black.

A plastic table had been set in the spacious yard, and there were chairs and a huge sunshade that cast a shadow all the way across the road. I said hello to my sister and brother-in-law, shook hands with both of them, and then my nephew came running in from somewhere, his haircut trim, wearing pleated shorts; I patted him on the head. Then I noticed—everyone in the yard was watching the two of us as if we were in some sort of cinematic scene, especially

Mama who was obviously waiting for me to hand him the money because the moment was ideal. But just as I was dipping my hand into my pocket, my nephew suddenly ran up the stairs and vanished into the upper story.

We sat at the table. Ate veal, potatoes, conversed, or rather, they talked and I listened.

At one point I pulled the 100-Deutschmark bill out and called for my nephew.

"He's upstairs, playing," said my sister. "Why don't you go up and give it to him there."

I went slowly up the stairs, entered a spacious room full of children's toys. He was in the middle of his kingdom, playing with a locomotive. I showed him the bill. He got right up, came over and took it.

He went to the door to his bedroom, stood on his tiptoes, pulled the door handle down, entered his room.

I waited and peeked. I could see him in there by the nightstand and he'd pulled out the drawer; in his hand he held a bundle of bills. He added mine to the top of the bundle, smoothed it with his tiny hand, put it back into the drawer and with both hands he slid it quietly closed.

"Whose money is that?" I asked when he came out.

"Mine," he walked by me.

I stood there among all the toys and watched him cheerily playing. Then I walked around the room, had a look at the framed needlepoints, the framed photograph of him when he was born, a picture of horses galloping their nostrils flaring.

I went nearer to the door and said, "Nephew?" He looked over at me as if I were about to give him another bill.

"Go check to see whether I'm in the bathroom," I said.

He got up, went off to the bathroom, and I walked slowly into his bedroom, pulled the drawer out quickly, took my 100-Deutschmark bill and shoved it into the back pocket of my pants. For a moment I had the feeling that I really ought to help myself to another. I barely managed to restrain myself. Out I went, shut the door behind me, but he was still nosing around the bathroom.

I crouched, played with the locomotive, used it to drive over other toys, dolls, my feet, everything in its path. Then he re-appeared from the bathroom and said, "You're not in there."

"Now I'm here," I said.

I played with him a little longer, drove toy cars around and made brrrrm, brrrrm noises. Then I went back down to the yard.

*

At the tram turnaround in Borongaj, while I was waiting for Džimi, a man had set up a stall and was selling Croatian flags, cassettes with the speeches of Dr. Franjo Tuđman; the items that were selling the best were little buckets with the words, "Pure Croatian Air."

I hadn't seen Džimi for a long time: his hairdo was the same, unlike mine, but his eyes looked as if he hadn't slept for years.

We hugged—right away I told him, to get it off my chest, that I wouldn't be able to return the other 40 Deutschmarks just yet. He brushed this off.

We each bought a beer at the minimarket; he paid for both because I was flat broke; I'd spent that 100-Deutschmark bill long before.

Džimi sipped his beer and looked up at his high-rise; from the stall near us we could hear Tuđman's voice.

"Have you been to any good shows?" I asked.

He said, "My old man was fired."

"Why?"

"I still have no clue," he shrugged. "Let's go up to my place."

"Wait for us to drink our beer," I said.

"Come on," he said. "Mama already asked me whether you're coming for dinner."

We ambled along, finishing our beer, left the bottles by the building and went up to the apartment. Džimi's mother greeted me from the bathroom; on the table she'd already set out a bowl full of chicken paprikash and two brimming glasses of elderberry juice.

"I saw you two coming," she said, "so I set out the dinner."

"I'd have a little paprikash myself," said Džimi.

"No you won't," she said. "You've already had enough."

This time, to my surprise, Džimi did what his mother asked and stayed sitting quietly at the table; he rotated his glass of juice in his hand.

"Have you been to Blue Moon?" I asked him, as I enjoyed the delicious meal.

He said, "Not for a hundred years."

"We could go on Friday," I said, dipping my soup spoon

in deep.

He shrugged.

"Let's go this Friday," I said. "We haven't been in ages."

He drank his juice, wiped his mouth with the back of his hand, and said, "Sure."

Then, once I'd finished my glass of juice, we went to his room, read comic strips, listened to music on his turntable; Jerry Lee Lewis was hopping around on the piano.

After a while the record stopped turning, Džimi dozed off, and I came to the end of the comic book; I got up and looked out the window. Then Džimi's little brother came into the apartment. I could hear him distinctly.

"Mama," he said.

"Yes, son?"

He asked, "Are we Serbs?"

"Yes we are, son," she said.

"All of us?" he asked.

She said, "All of us."

Then he banged the door with something and loudly declared, "Fuck!"

6

The morning sun rests on the bald pate of my grandfather.
He crouches in the yard: he is filling his colorful homespun
bag with potatoes, bacon, garlic, and a flask of water.

Father brought the bag from somewhere. I first used it
for carrying my slippers to school, but some of the kids from
the upper grades told me it was a bag for ladies and after
that I never took it with me again. Seeing that nobody was
using it, Granddad adopted it and carried it with him when
he went with the cattle to the forest.

I left the house and stood next to him. I was ready for
the journey. I hadn't shut my eyes that whole night after
hearing that I'd be going with Granddad up into the forest.
He'd whispered to me in confidence, "we are out to discover
a big secret, dig up buried treasure."

I could hardly wait for the sun to rise and usher light
into my little room. Probably fueled by my huge sense of
anticipation, the wardrobe where my clothes were hanging
opened all by itself that morning. Never had I dressed so fast.

Granddad told my mother and father, in passing, that
we were going off for a short hike up the mountain, to see

whether someone had knocked down and stolen our trees for firewood and, when they weren't looking, he sent me a sly wink.

Granddad took his hatchet, tossed his bag over his shoulder, and off we hiked uphill—Granddad first, and me, one step behind him. He strode along quickly for his age with short, energetic strides, but soon he tired and leaned on the first tree. He pretended he'd stopped because he had an itch on his back, so he had to scratch it on the tree, but I saw his strength was flagging. However, the more we walked, the more he seemed to gain in vigor, and at one point I was lagging as many as ten meters behind. He'd wait for me, then, again, the lag would grow.

I asked him, "When we find this treasure, will you buy me a guitar?"

He glanced over at me and said, "If you're good, you'll get an accordion. Guitars are for communists."

I said I'd be good and on we hiked. The sun followed us stubbornly, it baked the backs of our heads, sweat dripped down our brows. Granddad stopped, set the bag down and looked back toward our village. In the notch between two forested hills we could also see the village of Crni Lug. We savored the grand vista in silence and each time we stopped and turned to look back, our view was more breathtaking, enchanting—beauty that transcended our every gaze.

A short time later we passed by the bottomless pit into which the Ustashas had thrown people. Now the villagers threw in their dead animals or the dogs and cats they wanted to get rid of; the carcasses stank.

My granddad, who had himself thrown kittens into the pit at times, only remarked in passing, "Take care that one of the cattle doesn't fall in there."

I was always afraid of this pit surrounded by a grove of dark pines; sometimes from a distance I'd throw a stone in and listen for a few seconds to the rock that echoed as it fell and then I'd run quickly away.

On we hiked, Granddad was now choosing various shortcuts, but often these were quite overgrown, so he had to chop his way through with the hatchet and use it to push aside a twig that was about to slap him across the nose.

I walked a little behind him so any taut branch he hacked at wouldn't thwack me on the nose. The dense forest was forever devouring the pathways.

"We'll have a bite to eat here," Granddad stopped by a tree.

From his bag he took out the bacon, collected small stones, walled them into a circle, piled dry twigs inside it, lit it; the fire soon caught. He tore a hazelnut switch from a bush, sharpened it, and pushed it through the bacon rind.

With his other hand he tossed another few pieces of dry wood into the blaze, and when the fire burned down, he threw in the potatoes, covering them with the embers.

He held the bacon above, turning it slowly; it drizzled into the embers, raised sparks, sizzled, smelled delicious, set our mouths watering.

As we were tucking in, between two tasty, crunchy bites, something could be heard, sounds of some sort; Granddad cocked an ear, swallowed a mouthful only partly chewed, picked up his hatchet and gave a few full-throated yells, "Ohoo, hooo, ahoo, hoo!"

Again we listened, like one and the same body.

"An animal," he said. "And it's better to warn it that we're here than for us to bump into one another, then who knows what might happen," he said and ate.

He told me about a bear from the region. He said when it kills a human being it might become very dangerous because then it's no longer afraid of people; it loses its fear.

"So, where's that treasure?" I asked, just so he'd leave off talking about the bear.

"Nearly there," he said, his mouth full.

After we'd put out the fire and Granddad piled dirt on top of it, we hiked on. The forest became denser still, so dark and dense that we could no longer walk properly, but kept snagging on branches, stumbling over rocks, underbrush, clambering through a torrent of prickly, dark foliage. Granddad stood, pointed, smiled, and this meant we were nearing our destination. Emboldened, we forged on.

He walked just a little farther, then stood and with his right arm extended he gestured to an old tree next to a young tree, brimming with sap. By those two trees, like a father and son, or grandfather and grandson, jutted a big rock, round, covered in a green carpet of thick moss. Granddad's gaze strayed, and then, in his contemplation, one of his eyes turned back, at least that was how it seemed to me at the time.

Nothing could be heard aside from Granddad's breath, and when he held it and pondered, all I heard were the leaves whispering on the trees.

"That young tree wasn't here back then," said Granddad. "So that puzzled me a little, but I think we're in the right place."

He stood, moved his lips, and squinted as if counting the steps to his secret hiding place.

Slowly he walked toward the taciturn rock, knelt, scrabbled at something with his hands, reached for his hatchet and struck the ground with a few blows of the blade a meter or so from the rock. I knelt next to him. He didn't speak, he sank the hatchet deeper and deeper into the earth, stopped briefly and then used both hands to scoop up the dirt.

A little later the hatchet hit something hard; it rang, and I was certain this must be the metal chest containing the treasure. Granddad stopped, his ears—with long, gray hairs—flushed with blood and so did his face.

I, too, couldn't breathe from the excitement, I kept pressing my hand to my chest.

Up from the dirt Granddad pulled, or rather ripped out, a yellow-brown army-issue shirt, thoroughly rotten, around which was wound a belt, its buckle barely attached, and from the shirt he took a rifle. It was greasy, lubricated, and the butt in several places had rotted away, as if gnawed in the dirt by a mouse. Elated, Granddad held the rifle in both hands. He was breathing hard, and his breath sent him trembling.

"Whose rifle is that?" I asked him.

"Mine, from the war," he said and kissed it.

"And the secret buried treasure?" I said.

"This means more to me now than all the treasure in the world," he said, and pulled up a handful of grass to wipe the grease from the rifle.

Then he got up, laid his finger across his lips and told me I mustn't breathe a word about this to a soul in the village. He explained, while gazing at the rifle, that he had been thinking about retrieving it for several years, but now that wild animals had started coming closer to our house, down in the village, he decided to dig it up.

"So many years buried underground, yet it looks good as new," he said. "And I thought maybe it had already rotted away."

In the folds of the cloth shirt, he also found two magazines full of bullets. He slipped them into his pocket, stood up, cocked the gun, aimed at the closest tree, squeezed the trigger, but all we heard was the hammer falling slowly. He pulled the trigger a few more times and cocked it. By then the metal click of the hammer was growing more percussive. Then he loaded the gun, slung the hatchet from his belt, and off we set for home.

After a while, we spotted a deer, concealed by dense foliage, grazing near us on the meadow. It raised its head and then returned to grazing.

"I knew it," he whispered. "Deer are always grazing here."

He gestured for me to step back. I pressed up against a tree and covered my ears with my hands. Everything was still, with only my heart racing.

A shot.

Granddad shouted, "She's wounded, off you go after her!"

In confusion I ran over to him, he handed me the hatchet and shouted, "Faster!"

I dashed, peered around, and quickly spotted her; she had slunk into the bushes, retreated into a tangle of vines, her foreleg had buckled and, ensnared, she whimpered in pain. Granddad came after me and yelled, "Kill, by God's fucking blood, what're you waiting for?!"

I jumped, swung, struck it with the blade right in the middle of its head, and after that my hand flew toward it of its own accord with the bloodied hatchet.

I am walking around the apartment, twirling the brush through my hair, then I return to the mirror. I blow dry the tip of the pompadour with my hairdryer and watch how Eli can hardly move with that belly of hers—she's snagged by the table, the chairs, she grazes her books with her ass; this is wearing more and more on my nerves.

Later, she went into the bathroom, came back, sat heavily on the edge of the sofa.

"Do you know how awful this is," she ran her hands tenderly over her belly. "I can no longer even see my pee-pee place," she smiled.

This phrase of hers, "pee-pee place," was really getting on my nerves. Everything about her had been rubbing me the wrong way recently.

Then she said, "But, what matters is that the baby is doing well."

"How can you tell it's doing well?" I said, shaving my three-day stubble and working on my sideburns.

"What could be wrong, it's having a fine time swimming, pooping."

"Pooping?" I stopped shaving so I wouldn't nick myself.

"Yes, pooping," she laughed. "Why so surprised?"

"So where does the baby's poop go?"

"What about straight to your head?" she burst out laughing.

"What about straight to your head?" I said, shaving.

She went quiet, I felt her eyes on me, and she started to cry. I finished shaving, went over to her; she was perched on the bed, sobbing.

"What's wrong?" I hugged her.

"How could you say that to me?" she wriggled free of my embrace.

"What did I say?"

"That I have poop in my head," she said through tears.

"But you said it to me first."

"I was joking, but you meant it," she said, sniffling.

*

I missed a few trams when checking my reflection, unobtrusively, in their side windows; then I climbed up into one and rode it to the dorm; maybe there was a phone call or letter for me there, though I thought this was unlikely.

When I arrived, the fellow at the front desk with long hair who was forever stoned, always working away under the counter on a naive art painting on glass or, as he once told me, on naive surrealism, said there were no calls or letters, but that Afrim had been asking after me for a few days.

Then, as if he were doing me a huge favor, he invited me to lean over the counter and have a look at his nearly finished painting: a naked woman astride a cloud.

I nodded, just to nod, and the man at the front desk, with those little, bloodshot eyes of his, like small, glowing lamps, went on gazing for a time, pleased with himself, at his painting.

I asked him whether Afrim was up in his room. In response he simply shrugged, pondering his next brushstroke, and this irked me right away so off I went to Afrim's room without a goodbye. I knocked. Afrim was in his pajamas when he opened the door.

Warmly he shook my hand and began tidying his unaired room that smelled of tobacco and dirty socks.

"Sorry about the mess," he said and leaned under the bed.

I sat on the chair, waiting for him to be done.

"All I have is Cedevita orange powder to mix you a drink with," he said and carried a dusty sock, pinching it between his fingers as if it were a mouse.

"I am not thirsty," I said.

Afrim sat across from me, looked me over, and said, flattering me, "You look just like Elvis Presley."

I didn't say anything, with my eyes I just signaled that I was listening.

He said, "You know how I promised you a terrific job?"

"I do," I said.

"And when I make a promise, I keep it."

I nodded and looked at him.

"Do you have a passport?" he asked me.

"I do," I said.

"Sell it to me," he said. "I'll give you 60 Deutschmarks for it."

"What good will my passport do you?" I said.

"That's my business," he said. "Soon you'll have a brand-new country and a brand-new passport," he said.

After thinking about this briefly, I said, "Sure."

He reached into his pocket and handed me the 60 marks. I took them and turned them slowly in my hand.

"That's not all," he said. "For every red Yugoslav passport you bring me, you'll get another 60 marks."

I put the bills away in my pocket and immediately began thinking about who might give me their passport.

*

I am standing with Džimi at the very end of the bar at Kulušić and am thinking about a sentence I read somewhere a long time ago: Standing at a bar is the most beautiful sight in human existence. I can agree with that, at least this evening; it's been ages since I felt this fine.

I no longer have the pressure on my chest—haven't had it for weeks. Sometimes it crops up (I hope it won't tonight) but then it passes.

Džimi was drinking whisky and I was drinking beer and eyeing my pompadour in the mirror behind the bar—just like the good old days.

All this time I hadn't even realized how long my hair had grown; the pompadour was one of the largest I'd primped. Before I always had shorter hair in the back, a shaved neck, but now the hair on the back of my head was longer and covered my neck. I used up two small bottles of hairspray and made the front tip so sharp that I resembled a human unicorn. Džimi also remarked that I'd never had such a wild pompadour; his was ordinary, only his sideburns were bigger.

When Džimi came over, I thought he'd comment on the blond, buxom, perfumed girl who had walked by us just then, but instead he asked me, "Čarli, did you know I'm a Serb?"

"I did," I said.

He asked, "How?"

"Well, it says Momčilović on your front door."

He downed another whisky, suggested that the two of us sit in the armchairs, which, by some miracle, were still unoccupied.

He ordered yet another whisky and a beer for me.

Silent, he spun his glass in his hand; he began telling me about his father, how he had been wasting away since he was fired from Končar, and how his mother kept telling him to go to the hospital, but he flatly refused.

Then Džimi told me about the day when his father was stopped from entering the company building even though the workers there liked him; the doorman simply informed him he was banned.

He told me how people called them on the phone late at night, told them to go to Serbia, called them Chetniks.

Someone came to the entryway of their building and with a match or a cigarette lighter they burned and singed his family's surname on the building's intercom.

"And both my grandfathers were Partisans," he said.

After a few minutes of silence, he told me about his cousin, Miodrag, who lived in the village Džimi's father was from.

"He came by to see us the other day ... Apparently people are coming over from Serbia and arming folks in the Serbian villages with weapons ..."

He looked over at me, grim and pensive.

"Čarli," he said. "I think there will be war!"

I looked back at him, but in fact, through the smoke, I was looking at the speaker above his head. This story about the threat of war, here at that very moment at Kulušić, along with Bill Haley & His Comets who were booming "See You Later Alligator" from the speaker, came across as shaky and utterly unreal. And besides, I thought of Eli, the baby, the university, my life, but I didn't say to him, "Džimi, every day I'm at war."

I patted him affably on the shoulder.

"What fucking war!" I shrugged this off. "This will simmer down."

As we talked, Kulušić began to fill; with drinks in hand, we went to the dance floor. I danced, sipping my beer and turned, catching sight of familiar faces. The Vampires, Pinki 1, Pinki 2, and plenty of new young rockabilly fans sporting big pompadours, glistening with pomade. But I did not see a single one larger, more compact and wilder that night than mine.

I began dancing harder; Džimi, who was standing near me the whole time and sipping his drink, wandered off somewhere into the crowd.

I went looking for him and noticed him sitting on the wooden steps that led to the gallery. He'd fallen asleep there with his head dropped on his chest.

I left him sleeping and went on dancing and trying to spot a good-looking girl.

Rockabilly music had clearly become popular in town during the time I'd not been around, so now there were new girls here. The DJ was spinning Carl Perkins, Gene Vincent, Elvis, but also bands like The Clash, the Ramones.

I finished off my beer, left the bottle in the corner, began dancing and playing air guitar, faster and faster.

A dark-haired girl wearing a brown leather jacket with tassels immediately caught my eye; she was dancing up a storm, so I stopped to watch her in admiration—she twirled, disappeared, then reappeared.

"Angie" by the Rolling Stones began to play.

I went looking for her right away in the crowd just so nobody else would get there first and asked her for a dance. She said yes, immediately wrapped both arms around my neck. We danced, pressed together in the crush, the unbearable heat, pushed even closer together by the other bodies.

I was breathing so deeply that it was as if I were breathing for my own lungs and hers; I didn't know what to ask her, so I danced, hummed riffs from "Angie," and searched for the best opening line.

"If I may ask …" I finally whispered in her ear. "Who do you like more," I asked her, "the Beatles or the Stones?"

*

With Džimi, who'd had a refreshing nap on the stairs and was now sober, I set off on foot toward the central train station, with the idea of taking the night tram to Eli's apartment. Džimi decided he'd go with me as far as Volovčica and then across Borongaj to his building. At the train station Džimi bought a burek with meat; I wasn't hungry.

The Žitnjak tram arrived and we got on to the last, half-empty car; we found seats, Džimi ate his burek, and as we were passing the bus terminal, I remembered the question of passports.

"Džimi?" I looked over at him.

"Yes?" he said.

"Would you give me or sell me your passport?"

"What good would my passport do you?" he asked, taking care not to also eat the greasy paper.

"I'll give you 30 marks for it," I said.

For a while Džimi pondered this as he chewed his burek, then he said he'd rather not sell his.

I patted him on the shoulder and said, "No problem." At the next stop several guys got on the tram; they didn't look dangerous.

One of them, a good-looking blond guy, glanced at us, smiled, and headed our way. I thought he might have recognized me; I didn't recognize him. Behind him was another guy, tall with goggle eyes.

They asked me to stand for them, though there were plenty of empty seats on the tram. I didn't want trouble, so I stood right up. Džimi also stood, though they hadn't asked him to. But the two of them didn't take our seats. Instead, they blocked our way to the exit door, because, as we'd agreed, we were about to get off. When the door closed, the blond guy said, "Are you Serbs?"

"Nope," said Džimi.

"You have a pointy head," the blond guy looked me up and down with a grin. "I bet you're a Serb."

Then he suddenly grabbed me by the tip of my pompadour; I jerked it free of his grip, but a few hairs were left in his fist.

I fixed my pompadour—my facial expression, blank as if nothing particular had just happened; the blond guy made a move as if he were about to punch me in the head, and Džimi said, "Boys, don't!"

"You, fatso, shut up," said the goggle-eyed one.

Then the blond guy nabbed me by the chest and demanded my ID or passport.

"Wait, you're not cops, are you?" I said and tried to push his hand away but couldn't.

The blond guy grabbed my face with both hands, pulled me in toward his head; our noses touched.

"Hand over your papers!" he barked in my face.

The tram was just slowing to a stop and the door opened. Džimi suddenly shoved the two of them aside with the weight of his body, jumped out, tried to pull me out with him, but with both hands the blond guy held on hard to the hem of my jacket.

The other one helped the blond guy, so Džimi was holding me on one side and the two of them on the other, and they pulled me, and nearly stripped my leather jacket right over my head.

I tried to squirm out through the door, which was starting to close, received a blow to the head and was pulled back. I crouched on the floor of the tram and heard others running over; I covered my head, kidneys, and thought the blows would never stop.

At the next stop, Heinzelova, they picked me up like a rag doll and threw me out—one laughed and kicked me in the butt. I'd have suffered all of it, all the blows, but that kick to the butt . . .

It felt like a humiliation that would outlive me.

I fell onto the street, crawled over to the curb, wiped the blood off my face and began thinking about a pistol, a knife, a sharp piece of steel, any weapon at all; I imagined killing them one by one, and then pulling them up from the dead and killing them again. My head was buzzing; I sat on the street and began cooking up a plan for the next day. First I'd go to the hunting supply store and try to filch a pistol and bullets, and then I'd go looking for them around Zagreb, a hundred years if that's how long it took. And then I'd kill them all.

Soon I managed to quiet down, but kept thinking: if I don't do this tomorrow, I'll do it the next day, in a few days, one of these days. I remembered the phrase my father most often used for this sort of thing, when he wanted vengeance, "At least there are more days than sausages."

*

After ten minutes or so a fancy black car pulled up next to me.

"Doing OK?"

"Yes," I said, and clambered to my feet, barely able to stand.

"Should I take you to the emergency room?"

I got into the car, stunned wordless, and shut the door behind me; a grandfatherly man with thick, wavy, well-groomed hair was at the wheel.

"Were you hit by a car?" he asked.

"No," I said. "I fell."

"Where would you like me to take you?" he asked.

"Follow that tram," I suddenly pointed down the tracks.

"Which tram?" Surprised, he looked to where I was pointing.

"Drive along the tracks and you'll catch up with it," I spat out, in a tone that now sounded like a cross between a command and fury.

With an expression as if I were holding an invisible pistol to his head, he started driving along the tram tracks; he sped up and his remarkably large hands spun the steering wheel with skill.

"I'll murder them," I said.

"Who?" he asked, looking up, startled, first at me and then ahead.

"The ones who did this to me," barrages of gunfire were blasting from my mouth. "I want to see where they live so I can murder them tomorrow."

We drove by Eli's apartment and still hadn't seen the tram. At Žitnjak we finally caught up with it, parked at the turnaround, but there was nobody on board except the conductor, who was dozing.

Gramps stayed in the car, I got out, turned and peered all around. From the ruddy half-dark loomed several cranes, frozen mid-motion.

I cupped my hands in a funnel shape and shouted with all my might, "Where the fuck are you, you motherfuckers?!" and a cat that had been standing next to a nearby tree raced up the trunk and vanished into the leafy crown.

The tram conductor had stirred and was staring at me through the fogged-up window. I picked up a fallen branch, forked, and started toward the tram conductor to ask him whether he knew which stop the guys got off at. Probably thinking I intended to attack him, he grabbed a metal rod, opened the door and said, from above, "Whaddya want?"

"Where are they?" I said.

"Damned if I know," he said with a Bosnian accent.

I walked around, clutching the branch, passing something that looked like my shadow; there was nothing to be heard but a dog barking somewhere, and the tram that was finally starting up.

I flung the branch at the cranes, as if they were somehow

to blame, and got back into the car. Looking into the rearview mirror, I repeated, "I'll murder them."

"And who are they?" asked Gramps in a low voice.

"I don't know," I said. "But when I find out, I'll chop them into mincemeat," I growled through clenched teeth.

Then I thought of Džimi; I was thrilled that at least he got away.

Gramps kept watching me out of the corner of his eye. Like in a silent movie, his eyes followed my every movement.

Then he asked me softly, "Does it hurt?"

"A little," I said.

"By your wedding it will pass," he laughed and patted me on the shoulder. "That's what my dad used to tell me when I was little."

I sighed deeply and Gramps asked me, "Where to now?"

I didn't feel like going to Eli's apartment or my cramped student room, but I didn't know where I did feel like going.

As if reading my mind, he said, "Why don't we go for a drink somewhere and maybe you'd have a bite to eat?"

For a while I said nothing, as if I were thinking about what he'd said, but I was still obsessed with those guys.

Then I said, "Sure."

"What's open at this late hour?" he said and started his car.

I thought right away of the ćevap joint that worked all night, so I explained where it was.

Gramps loosened his tie with one hand and with the other he steered toward the center of town, and the road wound over the car's tires. "Do you work somewhere?" He spun the steering wheel.

"I'm a student . . . Can I open the window a crack?" I asked because I felt a need for fresh air.

"Go right ahead," he said. "You have the button there."

I found the button, opened the window a little and thrust my arm out; it gulped the fresh air.

"May I ask what you are studying?"

"Agriculture," I said.

He asked, "And how's that going?"

"Agriculture is not for me."

"My great grandson," he smiled, "wants to be an astronaut."

When we were waiting at the next traffic light, he said, "I don't know whether you'd be interested in a job with the police. You're young, healthy, intelligent, and I happen to know through a friend that the police are looking for capable people."

"I hate the police," I said.

"The police force is now ours," he said.

Then we arrived at the Square of the French Republic. Gramps slowed down and asked me where he should go. I pointed in the right direction and with the same finger explained where he could park. Nearby a man was walking two identical dogs; Gramps watched the dogs fondly as they romped, then he followed me.

We entered the ćevap joint; some ten meters before we walked in I tried to do something about my unruly hair and the cuts on my face; I must have looked a wreck.

The people inside were much like they'd been that time

when I first saw Eli—the only new face belonged to the buxom waitress. She kept smiling and bustling around. Gramps looked at her and shot me a sly wink.

We sat at an empty table; Gramps ordered tea with honey, I asked for a beer and ćevaps with a side of ajvar. Then I went to the toilets; I soaped up my hands, rinsed the drying blood off my face, freshened up.

When I returned to the table I tucked into the ćevaps.

"Do you live somewhere abroad?" I asked him, swirling the tip of a ćevap in the ajvar.

"Argentina," he said and squeezed the honey into his cup. "I haven't been back here for forty years."

I nodded, took a sip of the beer and looked over at the mirror where I'd first caught sight of Eli.

"The other day I went to see the Croatian president," he said. "During that war he fought for the Partisans and I was in the Ustashas, but we had a very nice conversation. He agrees that we must never again allow ourselves to be divided as we were then, and all of us who have been living abroad for years, who have the expertise, the resources, we should help this country of ours be our pride and joy," he said and slowly brought the rim of his teacup to his lips.

Now Gramps went to the toilet; when he returned, strains of the Lambada were coming from the radio so he danced a little as he passed, and this spurred applause from a few of the drunken patrons at the bar. One of them came right over and struck up a conversation; a few of the other men surrounded him, joining the lively banter. Gramps paid for a round of drinks for everybody at the ćevap joint; he came back over to me and sat.

Somebody said, "Thank you, Mr. American."

I thought this might insult him, but he just nodded with a smile. Then he looked out the window and said, "Ah, Zagreb is so beautiful. Buenos Aires is beautiful, but Zagreb is beautiful, too." He gestured, as if he couldn't come up with the words. I nodded as if in agreement.

"You aren't from Zagreb either, are you?" he said.

"No, I'm not," I said.

"So where are you from?"

I told him the name of our nearest town, and then, as I often added when asked, I said, "But I've already been in Zagreb for some time."

He had just started to sip his tea when he stopped, slowly set down his cup, and knit his shaggy gray brows.

"From that town, or from one of the outlying villages?" he asked.

Before I could reply, to my surprise he began listing our villages and among them mentioned mine.

"I'm from Žliba," I said. "So, you know that part of the country well?"

He smiled, "If your grandfather was an Ustasha, chances are I was his commander."

I wanted to say that my grandfather was, indeed, an Ustasha, yet spent the war years in Sarajevo, but I said, "As far as I know, a man named Điđi who rode a white horse was the commander there."

He smiled and said, "Yes, that's me."

✳

Granddad never liked talking much about the time his brothers were arrested and put to death. At the time, he was being held in prison in Gospić where his fate was touch and go, but he was saved by Miško the Roma's mother.

In one of the leather compartments in his briefcase that had been hidden in the attic there was a photocopied document; I think Granddad got it from a man who married one of Mama's cousins. The man had been a prominent Partisan and lived in Zagreb; I know that, at one time, he had helped with the paperwork for Uncle Tome from Rijeka so he could obtain a permit for carrying his pistol.

I once pleaded with Granddad, when we were out on a walk in the fields, just the two of us, to tell me something about the people from our village who called themselves the Crusaders. I lied and said I'd heard about them in my history class. He stopped, crossed his arms behind his back, stared into the dense forest that surrounded us on all sides, and said that not a one of the Ustashas was willing to surrender to the Partisans because each knew that this would mean almost certain death.

Then, he said, when the Independent State of Croatia collapsed, the Ustasha fighters removed the letter U from their caps and replaced it with a cross on which were inscribed, both horizontally and vertically, initials that stood for the oath, "For the honourable cross and golden freedom."

Along with other bands of Crusaders in the area, Granddad said—warming to the conversation, his facial expression changing with each sentence—his brothers pursued their guerilla campaign against the communists and Yugoslavia; their hope was that soon there would be a war between America and the Russians, America would pull together a block of Catholic countries consisting of Croatia, Austria, Hungary, and then Yugoslavia, he said, would simply fade away.

He looked down and closed his eyes, as if he were done forever with looking at the world.

Then I asked whether he knew what had happened to that Ustasha on the white horse. Granddad frowned, "As I heard it, he was surrounded where he was hiding in a dugout and killed himself with a hand grenade so he wouldn't fall into their hands."

THE DEPARTMENT FOR THE PROTECTION OF THE PEOPLE (OZNA) FOR CROATIA

MINISTRY OF PEOPLE'S DEFENCE OF FEDERAL YUGOSLAVIA
No. 1310
Zagreb, 23 November 1945

SUBJECT: Report on liquidation of a Crusader band

TO THE CENTRAL COMMITTEE OF THE COMMUNIST PARTY OF CROATIA

We are herein submitting a report on intelligence received on 23 November 1945.

In the forests above the village of Žliba, in the district of Lika, a band of Crusaders, cutthroats from the so-called Điđi Company, was liquidated. Among those liquidated were Luka Cvitunić (1919), Jandre Cvitunić (1920), Pave Cvitunić (1923), Joso Česmak (1921), and Drago Škudra (1918), all from the village of Žliba. According to the information at our disposal, the above took part in a massacre in the village of Crni Lug, when, on 15 July 1941, the Ustashas (of Điđi Company) murdered 52 people, including women, the elderly, children, and also took part in other murders. The group was active as the Crusaders, and over the last few months they have frequently attacked our officers, soldiers and sympathizers, hence in the evening hours of 22 October 1945 they broke into the home of Dane Lončar, president of the local organization of the People's Front, hanged him from a mulberry tree by the house, and on his sleeve they wrote that they would hang anyone else who touched him. On 14 November 1945, on the road by Crni Lug village, they ambushed Lieutenant Miloš Cvjetičanin and army doctor Olga Lehner, with him in the vehicle, and murdered both of them on the spot. A day later they attacked a lorry full of soldiers traveling along the same road, killing three soldiers and gravely wounding two others. According to the information at our disposal, they robbed and pillaged agricultural cooperatives, and on 23 November 1945 on the road near Kapela they stopped a bus that was transporting peasants to the Karlovac fair and confiscated their money and other property. Thereafter, in a violent scuffle over divvying up the money and the spoils, which erupted in the group's hideout, Mate Vučija was killed and Joso Česmak was slightly wounded in the arm. The band was uncovered and smashed when member Ivica Brbar betrayed them in return for a promise of freedom. We are reporting herein that Captain Jure Bajdakić, known as Điđi (Gornje Jasike, Travnik) is still hiding out in these forests. Before the war he worked as a sales clerk in Zagreb. As well as serving as commander, this villain perpetrated numerous murders and acts of torture by his own hand and rewarded those Ustashas who proposed the cruelest forms of torture with rakija, the gold teeth of those they'd murdered, and other loot. On 15 April 1943, Luka Cvitunić and Drago Škudra took our comrade Stipe Bilić prisoner in the forest above the village of Žliba, and Jure Bajdakić, aka Điđi, stabbed him in the neck, ordered him to sing Ustasha songs, and then slit his throat and threw him into the bottomless pit. According to the information at our disposal, Jure Bajdakić, aka Điđi, has several hideouts in the forest where he is living, and he has a ring of accomplices in the villages.

✳

The phone rang and wouldn't stop; must be my mother, I thought, only she can be this persistent and tiresome. I leaped out of bed and ran my hand over Eli's hair—she had also woken—went to the phone, picked up the receiver.

But it was someone from the dormitory. He said he had an urgent message for me; it wasn't the long-haired man at the front desk who painted pictures of naive surrealism, nor was it one of the other front desk staff whose voices I was more or less familiar with. Probably a student serving as a stand-in.

"What's the message?" I asked.

"Some men will be waiting for you at three o'clock at the Lika," he said. "I called you this morning, too, but nobody answered."

"What men?"

"They said they're from the region you're from."

I looked at the clock—the time was 2:20 p.m.

I dressed hastily and set off on the tram for the dorm, because the bar is right across the street from it.

After I'd arrived at the dorm, I went straight to the front desk. A long-haired guy, his face mousy gray, was cradling a guitar and tuning the strings in a way that grated. I entertained the sarcastic thought—the front desk apparently attracted art lovers.

I said hi and asked him what these men he'd called me about that morning looked like.

As he tuned the strings, he said, "Wearing uniforms."

"Police?" I said.

"No, Home Guard," he said.

When it was ten of three, I went over to the Lika and there was Zdravko, standing next to a parked white Golf.

He waved to me but continued talking with a man in the Golf. Zdravko was dressed in camouflage, and he had a pistol in a holster hanging from his belt. Next to him stood another man from my part of the country. He was wearing a camo jacket and jeans and was holding a Kalashnikov; I hadn't seen the man in the car before. He was wearing a raincoat. Zdravko took a letter from his pocket and walked toward me, his expression grave.

"Good that you came!" he bellowed. "I was just about to take this letter over to the dorm for you."

He hugged me with one arm and handed me the letter; I could see right away that it was from Mama.

Zdravko then pulled 50 Deutschmarks in bills from his pocket, unfolded them and delivered them to me.

"This is also from your old lady," he said.

✳

I glanced once more at the letter in my hand and went into the Lika.

As I was on my way in, I imagined Mama writing the letter. Who knows what all she'd gone on about.

I ordered a beer, took a sip and, standing there, I opened the letter. There was nobody at the bar except a fly and a skinny waiter who, lost in thought, was wiping a glass at the other end. He looked in my direction with a spaced-out sort of gaze. The only thing in the world he wasn't taking in, or so it seemed, was me. I took another sip and began reading:

Dear son we are well I gave Zdravko fifty marks to give to you so buy what you need. Try to finish up this diploma and then grab your girl and the child when it's born you're not twenty years old anymore and when the war is over we'll do up a proper wedding says Dad. The war is here and the police station is now ours no Serbian Orthodox police working there anymore they refused to put the Croatian coat of arms on their caps so they ran away and they're shooting at us from Crni Lug with mortar shells. Take care and we all are sending you our greetings.

I sat down at the nearest table, drank my beer and began thinking about going back to where I'm from, though Zdravko said I shouldn't, because they had plenty of men but no weapons.

I eyeballed the room. The waiter stared out the window. The fly buzzed. My eye quirked. Fear began to surge from my racing thoughts; panic grabbed hold of me and, with it, the feeling that the pressure in my chest would be back.

After a fresh gulp of beer, and then another, and then another beer, again I felt the urge to return, and before I left, I'd scrounge a machine gun somehow, bedeck myself with those shiny bandoliers; my father would probably respect me more if I came home like that.

And besides, hand on heart, my situation in life was not exactly wonderful; I was a failed student, so—a failure.

A person with no outlook whatsoever.

I was thinking, maybe the war was, in fact, the only way for me to achieve something in life—if I survived, of course. Fear gripped me again.

Yesterday Džimi's father died; a heart attack. When Džimi called to tell me, and I was gasping silently in shock on the other end of the line, he went cold, "Fuck it, that's life," but his voice on that last word did quaver a little. Then, on the verge of sobbing, he mumbled, "See ya," and hung up abruptly. I called him right back to tell him how terribly sorry I was, to try to console him, I dialed the number, the phone rang, but nobody picked up at the other end. I tried again ten minutes later. Now the phone was busy, and went on being busy, so I figured he'd deliberately taken the receiver off the hook.

A strong wind was gusting and the sound kept shifting. Dark clouds nudged each other across the sky.

Eli had just come back from the grocery store; she'd bought spaghetti for dinner. She took off her coat and walked around the apartment with both hands on her belly. Somehow, she managed to peel one leg of her nylons off a foot and was trailing the other around behind her like the shed skin of a snake.

She sat down next to me, kissed me, asked what I'd be wearing to the funeral.

"Nothing," I said, meaning I'd be going to Džimi's father's funeral dressed as I was—in my leather jacket, jeans, boots, with slicked-back hair full of dandruff—every so often it started itching something terrible and I'd slip my finger into the filthy nest and scratch and scratch, and there'd be greasy white gunk under my fingernail.

I paced around the apartment, pulled on my boots, stomped my feet a few times to get them on properly, checked my reflection in the windowpane (I looked like a ghost), kissed Eli and left.

I walked toward Mirogoj Cemetery, climbed up the grassy slope, and finally there I was.

I had been in Zagreb for such a long time, yet this was my first time seeing Mirogoj up close. I was surprised by how vast the cemetery was—magnificent, surrounded by high walls. I don't know why, but my first thought was that it reminded me of the Roman Empire.

I entered through the towering gateway, icy to the touch, strode into an unnatural stillness along the paved path framed by banks of candles, spotted Džimi surrounded by a few people in black, and approached slowly.

I shook hands and conveyed my condolences first to Džimi, with a strong hug, then to his mother and tear-stained brother. She kept staring at me with frozen gaze, as if seeing me for the first time, possibly dazed from sedatives.

Džimi assumed the role of head of household; with that pompadour of his, wearing a simple black suit, dark glasses, his pallor was ashen. But he was standing standing tall and summoned us with a broad sweep of the arm into the chamber where, on a stone bier, lay the open coffin with his dead father.

We stepped one by one around the coffin; Džimi's father had shrunk so much that he looked like a child who had aged suddenly.

We lined up again around the coffin; Džimi, his mother, and brother stood across from us. As I'd assumed, there was no priest. A scrawny man with a cankerous, red nose, probably an employee of the cemetery, went over to Džimi and whispered in his ear.

Džimi nodded, the man slowly lowered the coffin lid, opened a metallic gray door behind them in the wall, like the door of a giant bread oven. He turned a crank by the bier and the coffin moved slowly toward the opening. Džimi's brother began to wail; his voice under the high vaulted ceiling echoed like a cry broadcast over a megaphone. He started to chase after the coffin, lunging to stop it, but his mother and Džimi rushed to hold him back. He kicked at the floor and wriggled to pull free. Džimi was barely able to hoist him up, carry him. His tears streamed behind his dark glasses; with his brother in his arms he twisted like a wooden puppet on a string.

*

Back at Eli's apartment, I went straight from the front door to the bathroom.

I undressed, showered, looked for a minute or two in the fogged-up mirror. I was very thin; I'd never been fat, but now the upper part of my body showed the distinct claviature of ribs.

I splashed my face, came out naked in front of Eli who was deep into a book about child-rearing; she didn't even look up at me.

I walked by her, stroked her hair, scavenged a pair of her clean underpants from the cupboard as I no longer had any clean underwear of my own. I put on the striped pajamas of her late grandfather and lay down beside her. I lay there and stared blankly at the ceiling; Eli set her book down and looked over at me.

"How was it?" she asked, lifting first one then the other heavy breast under her bra.

"I cried more than when my grandfather died."

She looked at me with compassion, then suddenly she hugged me tightly and drew me to her breast. I lay for a time on her overly warm bosom that bore the smell of milk, I felt comfortable as she ran her fingers over my damp hair, down the back of my head.

I realized she was crying because she began, silently, to shake; her warm tears dripped onto my arm. I let her cry, but when she didn't stop, I got up and, furious, I asked her why she was crying.

"I don't know," she said. The murky room was reflected in her teardrop. "But I really, really need to cry."

*

I picked up the phone, called Džimi at his apartment, but nobody answered. The next day I called again; it was beginning to seem bizarre. Whenever I used to call, somebody would always pick up, most often his mother. Except, of course, the time when he called to tell me his father had died and after that didn't want to be disturbed.

I left the phone booth I'd been calling from and set off toward his building. I was on my way through the underpass by the central train station when I passed people wearing black uniforms. They were holding submachine guns with drum magazines, the kind that members of the Red Army carried in Second World War documentaries.

One of these fighters from the Croatian Defence Forces had fastened at least a dozen letter U pins to his beret; he was the only one holding an M-48—the same rifle my grandfather had used to kill himself—trailing it along drunkenly behind him the way a child trails a toy. Finally I emerged from the underpass, hopped onto the first tram flooded with dirty, uneven light and headed toward Borongaj. There were no seats available so I stood, leaning against the back window of the tram, and looked out.

As the tram trundled along, everything outside it acquired a different hue. The next sharp turn swung me to the side so I reached for a strap.

Again I stared out the window, sunglasses flashed and people seemed to be sending one another secret signals.

I hopped off the tram at the last stop and walked over to

Džimi's building. For a while I watched children playing on the grass between two buildings, shrieking with their little voices.

One had a chipped, old Pony bike with a car's steering wheel welded onto it— Zdravko had a bicycle like that once. Another boy was hiding in the branches of a verdant tree, imitating the barking of a dog.

With a glance I tried to spot Džimi's brother among them. I couldn't find him.

I walked toward the entryway to the building; the cool breeze felt good. There was always wind gusting around the huge high-rise, even in summer. I took the dilapidated elevator to the eleventh floor and arrived at Džimi's door.

Had a look. Must be the wrong floor. How could that be?

When I took the stairs to the floor below, assuming I must have taken the elevator to the twelfth floor by mistake, the name on the door there was "Kolar". What the fuck, I thought. I got back in the elevator and went back up to the floor I'd come to first, turned to have a look around, and now I was certain that this was Džimi's eleventh floor.

Again, I checked the door.

Yes . . . instead of "Momčilović" the name on the door was: "Oliviera". It couldn't be that he'd moved away and hadn't let me know, and now someone else was inside.

I knocked a little more loudly than usual, cocked an ear, heard some metallic sounds. Again I knocked, and with the palm of my other hand I channeled the sounds coming from inside the apartment toward my ear. I recognized Džimi's footsteps. I was so relieved to hear he was there.

He undid the latch on the door and gave me a nod; his face was pale and somehow bemused, like those people who wear glasses their whole life and suddenly take them off and squint. He turned, said I should close the door behind me and wait a minute; he went into the bathroom, all the while he seemed to be feigning aloofness. I closed the door, turned, and the first thing I observed from there in the front hall was the echo of vacancy. The apartment had been quite emptied, there weren't even any pictures on the walls.

I made my way awkwardly into the living room where there was a blue mat spread out on the floor and around it weights in various sizes as well as several exercise machines. The apartment had been transformed into a fitness gym; the air smelled of stale sweat.

Džimi came out of the bathroom; now I had a better look at him. As if he'd aged a little in the meantime—maybe because of his hair which had been trimmed quite short.

"What's going on?" I asked.

"Everything and nothing," he said, with uncharacteristic calm.

"Where are your mother and brother?" I asked.

He got up, turned to shut the door to the bathroom, then left it open a crack, but nothing in these movements made any sense.

"Mama and Zoran have gone to Belgrade; I stayed behind," he said, but his gaze was briefly separate from his face.

Then he told me, staring at the wall, that he'd had a bad

fight with his mother; she didn't want to stay in Zagreb, but he did want to stay; in the end he stormed out of the apartment, spent two days knocking around, sleeping on park benches. When he came back, the two of them had gone. He said they left him a message that they'd be staying with relatives in Serbia; he hadn't been in touch with them yet, nor had they with him.

"Call them," I said.

He said, "There's time."

Then he said I shouldn't call him Džimi anymore because he had a new name now. Then I thought of the brass plaque on the door—I hadn't had time to ask him about it—but he stood up abruptly, went to his cramped bedroom, brought out his pants, pulled a shiny new ID card out of the back pocket and handed it to me. His most recent photograph, in color, and beside it, in bold lettering, "Viktor Oliviera."

I took the ID and had a close look at it; bewildered, I looked over at Džimi.

"I don't get it," I said. "As far as I know, your name is Miloš."

He said, "That used to be my name. Now it's Viktor and please call me that in future."

As he uttered this, his voice coursed through him carrying an edge with it, especially when he said the words: Viktor Oliviera. As if he wanted to change not only his first and last name, but also the very timbre of his voice.

"No problem," I said.

So, as if we were taking a break from something neither he nor I cared to discuss any further, I glanced out of the corner of my left eye down through the window and caught sight of a truck that transfixed me. Džimi, sorry, Viktor, went to his room to return his ID and pants.

The yellow truck was still standing there, as if it had suddenly broken down at the traffic light. I took a closer look, there was no tarpaulin, only the four tall metal sides and from above, from the eleventh floor, everything was clear to see: there were people lying in the back. At first I thought they were tired, sleeping.

Then I noticed that the bodies were lying in totally unnatural positions and realized that these were, in fact, dead bodies.

I looked down and heard Džimi, as through a fog, saying from the next room that he was determined to exercise and lose weight, that this was the only thing he cared about in his life now. Even rockabilly or Elvis, he said, no longer interested him, just exercise and losing weight. He chanted this like a mantra: exercise and weight loss.

I listened to him, and at the same time I stared down at the truck, at the people, the corpses.

Finally the truck started up again and slowly merged in with the other vehicles on the road.

Also by Damir Karakaš
A *Paris Review* Best Book of 2024

"An astonishing read reminiscent of Boris Pasternak [and] Alexander Solzhenitsyn . . . Karakaš leads the reader into the individuals that make up the forces of history" — Robert Allen Papinchak, *Asymptote*

"A masterpiece . . . an event in Croatian modern literature" —*Vijenac*

"Dark, intoxicating reading from a literary wizard" —*Novi list*

"The reader's hair will frequently stand on end from pure aesthetic thrill" —Miljenko Jergović

"A novel of profound meaning and essential literary beauty" —*Večernji list*

DAMIR KARAKAŠ is an award-winning Croatian author, playwright, musician and journalist. He is the 2021 winner of the prestigious Meša Selimović award. Born in 1967 in the remote, mountainous region of Lika, he later studied law and agronomy in Zagreb. During the 1990s he worked as a war reporter from the front lines in Croatia, Bosnia, and Kosovo for national daily newspaper *Večernji list*. His novel CELEBRATION, published by Selkies House, was shortlisted for the 2025 European Bank for Reconstruction and Development Literature Prize.

ELLEN ELIAS-BURSAĆ is an award-winning translator of Bosnian, Croatian, and Serbian, who has served as the president of the American Literary Translators' Association. Between 1972 and 1990 she lived in Zagreb and for six years she worked in the English Translation Unit of the International Criminal Tribunal for the former Yugoslavia in The Hague, Netherlands. She is the translator of celebrated authors including Dubravka Ugrešić and Daša Drndić, author of *Trieste*.